About the author

Jane Burdiak lives in Bukinghamshire and is married with four sons. She works in a large comprehensive school as a food technology teacher, enjoying the challenge of a demanding and stimulating environment. *Domestic Science* is her second book to be published.

DOMESTIC SCIENCE

For
Julie Isabella Friell
1960 – 2008

Jane Burdiak

DOMESTIC SCIENCE

To Simon
Best wishes
Jane Burdiak

AUSTIN MACAULEY

A CIP catalogue record for this title is available from the British Library.

ISBN 978 1 84963 053 5

www.austinmacauley.com

First Published (2011)
Austin & Macauley Publishers Ltd.
25 Canada Square
Canary Wharf
London
E14 5LB

Printed & Bound in Great Britain

ACKNOWLEDGEMENTS

Special thanks to my friends Judy and Mandy, who have been with me all the way, and above all, to Elaine, who provided her invaluable technical expertise.

BE-RO illustrations used with permission from Premier Food Group Limited. And one line from *The Road to the Isles*.

January

The three books lay on the counter. The librarian swiped the bar codes on the front of each. A mouth of red light lit up in the hand-held scanner and her eyes travelled across the monitor to her right. She remarked on the covers, implying that there was something about them that linked, and indeed there was. The quiet muted colours and the subtle blurry images were nostalgic and inviting. She had chosen two of them for her husband three weeks earlier. The third book had been hers and she had hoped to finish it in the Christmas holiday. She had first started it in the summer on the flight back from Kafelonia, bored with the free newspaper placed inconveniently on her seat. As if there is space for reading a broadsheet newspaper on a package holiday flight.

"They say you can't judge a book by its cover," she said.

The librarian smiled, agreeing.

"I always judge a book by its cover," she continued. "It is what makes me pick it up in the first place." She usually chose paperbacks because they were lighter, easier to carry home and easier to hold. She would pull up a chair beside the revolving bookcase and gently spin the shelves until she came across a book that took her fancy. Sometimes she came across a book that she had read before. She always remembered the covers. Like old friends, she picked them up and turned a page, remembering. Why she chose books for her husband she never knew. He was perfectly capable. It had become a habit, a bad habit.

It had not been her intention to dismantle the tree. It just happened. Her husband was in the garden having a bonfire, taking advantage of the still, black night, and she was at a loose end. It had been a lovely tree, thick with spindles. Even on New Year's Day it didn't look tired. Reluctantly, she collected the carrier bags from the wardrobe and carefully stored the decorations for another year, returning the glass baubles to their vacuum-formed moulds and the fairy lights to their special box, weaving the wires around the cardboard tray. She was glad that she was alone. Even though her children were now in their twenties, she had never liked them to witness the harsh reality of ending the magic. Armed with a black sack and the secateurs, she began to remove the branches, making it easier to lift outside – never a problem when brought indoors because the white net had kept the branches under control. But, once cut, the branches exploded into the dining room, filling it with hazy forest and earthy pine. She questioned bringing a tree into the house. Surely a bizarre thing to do? Effortlessly the secateurs cut cleanly into the bark. She placed the branches in the sack. The tree, which only an hour earlier was spangled and dizzy with light, looked torn and desperate. She took its disfigured awkwardness outside to stand and shiver. The bonfire, reluctant at first to start, had leapt into life. She could see her husband silhouetted against the glittering sparks and licking flames.

A bitterly cold day had been forecast. Local news had brought reports of gritting lorries working round the clock and isobars tightly packed, the temperature hovering around zero, but feeling much colder in the strong easterly wind.

" Let's walk to The Black Horse," she said to her son, "and have lunch."

They took to the path wrapped against the icy wind and speckles of sleet. It was called The Railway Walk and long ago it had been the railway, prosperous and bustling, not as it was now, devoid of activity and lifeless. Slippery brown leaves had gathered and collected along the tarmac edges. Nettles, decaying, dark and waterlogged, swayed and leaned. Set back, on either side of the path, hawthorns glistened with beads of melting hoarfrost, their black branches bending in the wind. They ignored the dank and dreary outlook, walking briskly, determined not to succumb to the atrocious conditions. Log fires were an added incentive and the warmth greeted them as they opened the door. Well worth the effort, she thought. They chose a table and draped their hats, gloves and scarves over the red-hot radiator, ready for the journey home. The waitress suggested that it was false economy to have two glasses of wine, that it was more economical in the end to have a bottle. She was easily persuaded. In fact, she didn't need persuading. They both chose the game pie. It sounded much more interesting than pan-fried chicken on a bed of rocket and it was seasonal, hot and warming. The wine mulled and blurred the walk back, even though the scarves, hats and gloves offered intense, deep heat before the icy blast penetrated on the other side of the door.

Saturday too was cold. As she waited on the platform a funnel of wind ripped through the station, snatching her hair and whipping it about. Even though she knew she would be cold to start the day she dressed meanly. She didn't want accessories and her coat to hinder. She was going shopping and knew that by twelve she would be throbbing with heat, horribly hot and irritated with excess baggage.

She went to Liberty's, her favourite shop. Although she looked at the bags and the scarves on the ground floor she had gone to look at the fabrics on the third floor. The wooden staircase was just as she remembered, the banisters, old and over time smoothed with hands, comfortably worn. No neon, no plastic, no hideous shop fittings and if there were and there probably were, they were discreet. She imagined she smelled polish, polish out of a round tin, rubbed deep and buffed with yellow lightness. Even as a student she had frequented the shop. She liked the atmosphere and the feeling, she didn't have to buy anything. It was like another time. Since her last visit, the area devoted to fabrics had been reduced to a fraction and the selection to a minimum. She sauntered round the open Elizabethan gallery, lightly taking her fingers over floral lawns that caught her eye and a basket of lavender bags tactile and inviting. She couldn't resist. Beautifully made and fat with dried flower heads that rubbed against each other when she squeezed one in her hand. The smell lingered, fragrant and summery. It was about the only thing she could afford and, looking back, she should have bought one. Everything was hugely expensive. She went down a floor to ladies' fashions. A black silk voile dress with a flocked spot caught her attention. She put her glasses on and scrutinized the topstitching, rows and rows of it. She could find no faults. She examined the placket and the tabs on the cuff and, horror of horrors, there was a band of fraying silk on the edge of the cuff. Surely a mistake. She checked the other cuff nearest the wall. The same. She lifted the hanger off the rail. The neck too had the same distressed look. A design fault. Definitely a design fault, she concluded. That was why it was still hanging there, reduced to£469.95. A snip.

It was Sunday. The impending start of term overshadowed her day, creeping in and out of her thoughts. It was never far away. She had to remember to take ingredients for spaghetti bolognaise and put a partly squeezed tube of tomato purée on the kitchen table to remind her. The low January sun poured in, bright and light, showing up the smears and the flaws. She looked in the mirror. Every hair on her face was there to see, exposed. Removing her glasses, she hoped that the image, how others would see her, was lessened. Those with good young eyes would see. Children were perceptive and they missed nothing.

Slowly the darkness seeped away and was replaced by looming grey shapes. Soon it would be time to get up. It was only in the long summer holiday that a normal sleep pattern resumed. Between two and three she woke and from then on found sleep impossible. She would lie awake thinking and planning her day or the week ahead. She knew that she would be fine when she walked into her classroom. She had a light purposeful air and spent her time distributing booklets and sheets of paper and packets of crayons. She welcomed the pupils at her door. Now, how many weeks was it until the next holiday?

She appreciated that writing an evaluation about a pizza or a shepherd's pie was not terribly exciting and it wasn't long before an interesting conversation about body piercing commenced, much more interesting to a fifteen year old. It was mainly between three boys but she could see that several others were listening, wanting to join in but feeling awkward and embarrassed, not having the nerve or the confidence of their peers. Her newly found half brother had emailed the most dreadful images of body piercing with a comment about being thankful that their children had not gone down that path. She, too, was thankful. She had to have her pennyworth and say what she thought on the subject. She wasn't bothered if they weren't interested. But they were and were keen to hear what she had to say. Whether it would make any difference, who knows? Maybe in years to come when they were grown up and had responsibilities. She told them about the time on the underground, on the Piccadilly Line between Cockfosters and Euston. It was sunny and about four in the afternoon. There were only two other people in the carriage. At Arnos Grove three punks boarded the train with matching dogs that snarled and barked and strained at their studded-leather leads. Long strands of saliva drooled from their foaming mouths. Their loose lips stretched tight, baring fangs and yellow teeth. The men didn't sit down. Menacingly they stood by the doors and allowed their dogs to jump up and claw at the advertisements above the door. One Alsatian reached easily, its claws scraping over the glass as its paws returned to the floor. The pit bull snarled. The men were smoking and had no regard for the signs, which said no smoking.

She wanted to look, but she didn't want to look just in case they thought she was staring, which she was. They were wild and hideous. The hair she could cope with, but their faces were punctured with studs and rings and pins and chains. She knew little about body piercing, only what she had seen and that a stud had damaged her son's perfect teeth. At the time he wouldn't be told. She told the boys this. She said that from what she had seen people abroad didn't go in for body piercing or tattoos, for that matter. Just imagine being old and needing a hip replacement and the once pink pert skin needled into pictures but now withered and grey, hanging creepy skin, like a spent balloon, wizened and

17

misshapen. Then the subject changed to hairy legs. Sandra, who so far had been quietly getting on with her work, felt that men should wax their legs. The boys were outraged. What, wax their legs? With that Harry jumped off his stool and rolled up his trouser leg, then, even more surprisingly, so did Karl. Everyone laughed, including her. It was time to go home.

Barely into the first week back from the Christmas holidays, there had been vandalism in the boys' toilets and a memo had followed wanting to know which pupil had been allowed to leave the classroom.

She didn't like driving in the dark. She had lost her confidence. It wasn't because she didn't like driving and it wasn't because she couldn't see and it wasn't because she didn't like the dark. It was because, in the dark, normal everyday things like lorries and cars, trees and buildings took on new shapes and the whole time, while she was driving, she would try to imagine what she was seeing and try to see the images she would see in the daylight. A lorry overtaking another lorry was a ghastly big black hulking shape. No longer a lorry. Hedgerows and trees were the same. This prayed on her mind, her concentration diverted, and it was almost a relief when the eerie grey dispersed to be replaced with a fuzzy morning light until real daylight returned. Driving on the motorway, especially to the airport, the road was lit; she could cope with that until junction ten loomed. It had been clear when she left home at four thirty but the visibility had changed and when back on the main road her anxiety returned. She could see the airport lit up, then suddenly the road dipped. A pocket of fog obscured the lights, like a dimmer switch turning them off. Concentrate, concentrate, concentrate.

Exam invigilation was one of those things that had to be endured; at all times attentive to pupils' needs, a piece of paper here, a calculator there. A trip to the toilet, standing guard outside till the chain was flushed. It was undoubtedly boring but she devised things to do, which were discreet and kept her entertained. Pelvic floor tilts and stretching her spine as though a piece of string was pulling her towards the lofty heights of the cricket nets, her chin tucked in, her bum tucked in, went unnoticed. If she was fortunate enough to be at the back of the hall, then all manner of exercises could ensue. However, most of the time she would be visible and unable to touch her toes twenty times. In the quiet unnatural silence a number of activities could be carried out, mainly involving counting. Counting bricks was one, until the whole wall became one big brick. Left-handed writers, pupils wearing trainers, pupils with a diamond earring, how many ethnic pupils in a row? But once she had the data how would she store it? She taught twenty year eleven pupils, but she had in the past probably taught them all at one stage or another. In their so far short careers, many, the pits in year nine, had matured. They had grown up and lost their teenage angst. They were polite and said "Hello, Miss."

Apart from going to the building society she wanted to get some mug trees. Her high street was littered with charity shops and she felt sure that she would be successful. The local hospice shop had one in the window displayed next to a kitchen roll holder. Although pleased to have found one mug tree, she knew that she would need another and tried the Age Concern shop. There was one but it was being used to display a set of random mugs. Carefully she removed the mugs and took the mug tree to the counter.

"It hasn't got a price on it," the charitable lady said.

"No," she replied.

"It's a pound," she continued.

She put it in her carrier bag next to her previous purchase. At last, her necklaces would be organized. For years she had laid them on top of her chest of drawers. She didn't want them in jewellery boxes, out of sight, out of mind and she didn't like the existing tree arrangements. They were too fussy and not her style and they gathered dust. It was true that how her necklaces were, they gathered dust, but at least she could see them all at once. Really she would have liked something to hang inside the wardrobe door, like a tie rack but a jewellery rack instead, instantly accessible. She kept thinking about the kitchen towel holder. It stood taller than a mug tree and would be more useful for longer chunkier necklaces. She could buy some interesting turned dowel and drill two holes. She knew it would work. Would it still be for sale next week?

Satisfied with her purchases, she waited patiently in the queue in the building society. The queue was endless. Why couldn't old people go to the bank during the week. Twice, she had called in to check the queue.

After half an hour, as she was leaving, she met a friend. She had seen her friend's mother first. Her daughter, once tall and robust was a shell of her former self. Strangely she looked older than her mother, supported by two walking sticks. What had happened? Lymphoma had been diagnosed some months ago. Knowing how long they would be waiting, she sat with her friend to catch up. Julie looked small and childlike. Her hands trembled uncontrollably as she searched in her bag for the cheque that she was about to pay in. She took her handbag out of a pink Nike shoe bag.

"I've got one of those bags. I got it when I did the Race for Life," she said to Julie.

Julie laughed. She too had done the Race for Life but at the time hadn't realised that she was running for herself. Soon after the race, she was very, very ill. Nearly an hour had passed and the queue stretched to the shop next door. Glad to be outside in the fresh air, she walked home briskly, the image of her friend fixed in her mind.

It had been the week of marking the mock exam papers to see what the pupils had remembered and gauge if they had been listening and paying attention in revision lessons. She sat on the edge of the settee, facing her husband and turned all the papers to question one. She managed an hour before absolute boredom set in and sleep insisted. Until they were done that was how they were marked, somewhere between lethargy and determination, when some good news on Thursday set her adrenalin running and her nervous energy made her finish them just as her husband came home.

"Just two more and I'll make the tea," she called as she marked furiously in red pen. The elation of getting to the end of question nine was immense. Good, she thought. She could watch television without feeling guilty.

What possesses children to smear syrup all over the door handle and the gas box emergency button?

"It was a dare. Jenny dared me," she said when she owned up. And with a name like Livi! That was not the only thing that day. The night before, graffiti had been sprayed on the school walls.

"Have you seen the graffiti, Miss?"

"No I haven't," she said. "I arrived this morning when it was dark."

"I'll show you, Miss."

In an instant the phone was out and on a screen the size of a postage stamp, there it was. Thick hard black lines against the white stippled wall. Not even "good" graffiti.

Saturday, 19th January had finally come round. She sat in the car. Had she got everything? She had got her mother and the roses tied with a tartan ribbon. She was wearing her coat and in spite of the howling wind and threat of rain it was surprisingly warm and she did not need gloves and a scarf. Her mother, however, would not see her as being properly dressed without, and, for her mother's sake, she went back in and grabbed a scarf off the hook in the hall and a pair of gloves tucked in the corner on the third stair up. Her mother had sat in the hall on top of the box used to store the drum kit stands for at least eighteen months. Gradually she had got moved into the corner, coats obscuring her. Although she was out of sight, she was not out of mind.

She stood beside the freshly dug plot, the chalky earth piled up on a piece of plastic sheet beside. She hadn't told anyone her plans for the morning. Ideally, she would have liked her sister to have been there but could see that her latest building renovation filled her weekends. She had expected the churchyard to be desolate, with only a robin for company, and that she would be tearful and melancholy. But no, it wasn't. There was Frank, who had dug the hole, standing with his hands on his hips, his jacket over his blue boiler suit and knee pads protecting his dodgy arthritic knees. Then Peter came along. Why, she didn't know. But she got the feeling that he had had a soft spot for her mother. It was something that he said. "She had a few years to herself then. That's what she wanted. Your father gave her the run around." You could say that, she thought to herself. Frank got on his hands and knees and took the oak casket from her, placing it carefully in the neat rectangular hole. On top she placed a single red rose. Frank and Peter joined in with the prayers, after which she scattered a handful of earth over her mother. Amen. She went with the vicar into the church to sort out the paperwork. They entered by a small wooden door that opened into the choir stalls between where the altos and the tenors would have stood. Ladies were arranging anemones in vases. She knew the church well, from her days as a chorister and Sunday school teacher. It was familiar, and hadn't changed in forty years. It was quiet and peaceful and had a certain smell. Crabtree and Evelyn brought out a fragrance called "Damask", sadly discontinued. It was exactly the smell of the blue cassock she used to wear. In that short time the weather had changed. The ancient yew trees leaned in the wind, rain stung her face. Frank had returned the soil and the turf to the plot and placed her roses on top.

A wandering grassy path between the gravestones led to a gate in the far corner of the churchyard. To her, when she was small, the vicarage was stately and imposing with its gravel path and sash windows either side of the dark green front door. Its garden was big, and extended all round the house. It hosted the annual village fetes and Sunday school parties. Bunting fluttering from tree to tree, sawdust bran tubs and "what's the time Mr Wolf", sitting cross-legged on the grass, when ladies wore hats and white gloves. She remembered once being entered in the fancy dress competition. She had been dressed as a rocket. Her father had made the structure, determined that she should win. It was made out of some sort of plastic and the smell of it was disgusting in the warm afternoon sun. It was fairly rigid and very close fitting. Her arms had to be clamped to her sides and it was difficult to walk. All the entrants met at the far end of the village and rode in style on a farm trailer, pulled by a tractor to the vicarage. It was a colourful scene. People lined the road and cheered and waved. It was when summers were summery. The older Sunday school children met in the vicarage for their lessons, instead of the church. She remembered the study, sitting, along with others the same age as her in a semi-circle around the Almighty, powerful and controlling, listening to him intently, hanging on to every word. She had to admit that she didn't doubt what he said, she didn't question. It was cosy and nice and she liked the security that it gave her. Sometimes there was a glass of orange and a biscuit. Even in her early teens she had dreams of becoming a missionary, of striding out into the wild African jungle and taming the tribes. Now in her cynical old age she saw how vulnerable she had been, how naïve and gullible. He was a respected member of the community, a devout theologian. Her mother had obviously thought it was the right thing to do, to send her daughter to be indoctrinated for hours every Sunday. It was what she had known as a child. In 1926 she had been presented with a framed certificate for one hundred percent attendance. It had turned up in recent years and been sent from Scotland. Her mother had not been too interested. She still had all her Sunday school prizes, always books. One book in particular stood out in her mind, called "Stories from Holy Writ" given to her when she was ten, a hardback with a plain taupe cover. How dull and boring it looked. Although accepted graciously, she had never read them. But it didn't seem right somehow to tear out the decorated scrolled label, for excellent attendance, and throw them away. So their fading spines continue to sit on the bookshelf gathering dust. Her father didn't care about the church, he couldn't stand the place or the people who went to pray. For him, it was a convenient way of getting rid of her for a few hours on a Sunday. Peter had asked where her father's ashes were, obviously expecting them to be nearby. She said that they weren't and no, she didn't know where they were, and that he did not deserve to be buried in the churchyard. Peter understood.

Beyond the vicarage were the Meads, a patchwork of meadows divided by brooks, low lying and, in places, marshy. Milkmaids and kingcups thrived in the spring. Miniature pools of water lay where hooves had stood too long. Some fields were accessed by stiles but most were reached with a leap across the brook. This area of freedom provided unending fun all the year round, from collecting frog spawn in the spring to finding the longest icicle in the winter. It was when winters were wintry.

In the afternoon she went back to buy the kitchen roll holder. In disbelief, she peered in. The shelf where it had sat last week was empty.

She would wring the dishcloth tight like a rope under the hot running tap then tease it out and run it in her hand along the washing line to clean it. She would look at the cloth: a grey line, as she had thought. Smoke from roaring garden fires left their mark. She had to admit that hanging out the washing was her obsession. Even before it got to the line it was sorted into an order, her on hands and knees on the kitchen floor. She would empty the contents of the washing machine onto the floor and begin to sort. Sometimes she put all the things that needed one peg at the bottom of the basket so that they were hung out last, and then sometimes she wanted to get all the small things hung out first, so they went on the top of the pile. Socks she put into pairs. She could not hang out odd socks that didn't have a friend and she could not hang them on their own. Odd socks were hung on the radiator rack in the kitchen until they dried. Sometimes she classified the washing out in colours, starting with the deepest and going to the lightest – or bands of colour, all the blues, all the greens. Sometimes she hung it out in size going from the largest to the smallest. She had two props, their state of decay similar. Neither was long enough and both threatened to snap in two. Each had a V-shape cut out to support the washing line. Once, her mother had offered her a modern aluminium prop that could extend and retract. She declined her generosity claiming that she was happy with what she had. Really, she would have liked the prop but was too proud to say. She positioned the prop between things that would not get wrapped round it and get ripped on the rough wood. When she reached the back door she would look back at the fluttering washing as if it were a work of art, to be admired. She always knew when someone else hung it out. Trousers would be upside down, hung by their hems, socks on their own, sheets would hang longer on one side than another. Seeing it all random and haphazard was difficult to cope with. Bringing it in again was also a performance. Socks were balled while still pegged on the line, everything was folded to reduce the ironing, pegs placed in the peg bag, not mixed up with the clothes.

She knew she was irrational, it was silly but she couldn't help it. However, she failed miserably when it came to putting it away. Little piles of ironing would sit around from week to week, on the table, on the landing, never reaching the drawers and wardrobe. When her children lived at home she would deposit their piles of clothes at each bedroom door, like a hotel service.

She was wrapped in a shroud. Somehow it was a she. The bundle was too slight to be a he. She assumed her to be dead. She turned away and then looked back. A curtain, a dull stained curtain had been drawn across. It hung from the ceiling and hung smoothly without folds. Roughly in the middle there was a small three-cornered tear and through it she could see a face, with small elfin features. The face did not have a nose, just a raw gaping hole where her nose had been ,and rough black blood had dried around the torn flesh.
She woke up from her feverish nightmare, glad to be getting up.

No sooner had the GCSE marks been recorded on the database than it was time to start the cycle of the year nine internal exams. Apart from counting bricks and pelvic floor exercises it had freed up her week, only to be paid back in her own time with the marking of the wretched papers. She had sixty-five papers to mark and she marked them all through gritted teeth. The final marks were mediocre. 'Dizine' she could cope with, but on reading 'lickwish' and 'carrout' she gave up.

Three times this week tears had filled her eyes. A pupil who had been in her class just before Christmas had died. She had finally lost her fight for life just days before her fourteenth birthday as reported in the local paper on Tuesday evening. An impromptu assembly on Monday morning brought tears to her eyes. Many pupils were clearly distressed and cried openly, their sobs echoing around the vastness of the theatre. All were respectful, filing quietly into seats and not letting them bang noisily when they were asked to stand and remember their friend. She thought about Rachel, her smiling face and her courage. She thought about Rachel's last lesson with her. Alive in her mind she could see Rachel perched on a stool, decorating a cake for her brother's birthday, never knowing when it would suddenly end, as she knew it would. Had she taken a picture of Rachel's cake? She could not remember for sure. Although she was able, Rachel was in a group where most of the pupils had special educational needs or were just plain naughty. A library book had been mislaid and caused her to look in the 'research' box to see if it was there. Near the top of the box was the picture. She was glad. The cake had been carefully decorated with white glacé icing and chocolate chips. She had placed two plastic aeroplanes each side of her brother's name. Around the cake she had wrapped a birthday frill. Why hadn't she given Rachel a merit for her cake? That would be forever on her mind.

She had taken to going to the cinema with her two friends. They took advantage of it being bargain Tuesday. The plan was to go on the way home from school. They each knew that once they were home it was too easy not to bother going out again. Last week it had been "St. Trinian's". The film this week was "The Kite Runner". She had not expected it to be subtitled, but hearing the Afghan language added to the drama and the tension: it heightened her awareness to the awfulness, the ruthlessness and the madness of war. It wasn't from some far off time. It was now. Now, at that very minute, living in fear of the Taliban was still happening. There were still children like Amir and Hassan, wondering why they were living in terror and uncertainty. Truly moved, she blinked away her silent tears.

February

Another letter arrived in the post. Her manuscript, as it was known in the publishing world, had gone to the next stage in the process. She was so excited she could not contain herself. When she had a space in her day she thought about it. She had started writing about two years ago and the words had just flowed. Not once was it daunting or a chore. She didn't especially set out to write a book, she just wanted to get her thoughts down on paper, to get things off her chest. The liberating experience was hard to resist and so the words accumulated.

Almost incidental compared with the other two, the third time for tears was when the turn-up of her trousers became caught on a stool. She went to get off the stool when it lurched and fell on the back of her leg, just above the ankle. She winced and was cross with herself that such a silly accident had happened. She felt that the navy bruise the next day had justified her tears.

The pupils sat round watching her create some new bread ideas for children. She showed them how to make hedgehogs and dough ball flowers.

"You had that hair band on last week, Miss."

"Yes I did," she replied, knowing full well that she did and also the reason why. She was not going to tell the likes of Livi why. The accusation was distracting. She always made a mental note of what she had worn the previous week since a boy had said "You had that on last Tuesday, Miss," and another had told her that her apron didn't match her colour scheme. On Friday she would definitely not be wearing anything brown, knowing that she would be limping round Tesco at the end of the day, her feet killing her in her black shoes. She saw her flirtation with writing as a means of sitting down. Her whole day, apart from driving the car, was spent standing up. During the day her feet increased in size and her shoes, comfortable at seven in the morning, were tight and uncomfortable by lunchtime. At times, she longed to sit down.

For some time now she had wanted to see the statue of Christ towering over Rio de Janeiro. She had pored over the brochures back in October, but the plan had been shelved when the gas boiler needed replacing. By the end of January the summer holidays were once again on the agenda. She said to Graham and Angela at the local travel agents that arranging a holiday had to be one of the worst jobs in the year. It was comforting to hear them say that it was a pleasure to help and offer her a coffee to relax and calm her. She thanked them but declined their generosity. It would make her hotter than ever. She did not enjoy it at all and loathed giving up her precious time. To soften the blow, she had called into the travel agents during the week to get the ball rolling. Then, after an hour on Saturday morning, sitting tall on a swivel chair, her arms leaning on the counter, politely agreeing and nodding her head, it was all done and dusted. Light as a feather, she got on with the rest of her day.

A programme on Saturday evening prompted her to email Douglas. The programme, called Ten Pound Poms, was about emigrating to Australia during the fifties and sixties. Douglas was her half brother and had left with his mother on the Arcadia in September 1949. Then she wrote a "real" letter to the French Embassy wanting to know the addresses of all the Town Halls of the French channel ports during the thirties and forties. She planned to write to each to find out if Douglas's mother and her father had married, as Douglas had been led to believe. It didn't matter to her if they had or they hadn't. She just wanted to know.

The cortège was passing the school and pupils were invited to stand on the verge and say goodbye to Rachel. She stood along with her group. It was a blousy day, bright and gusty. The grass glistened with the earlier heavy rain. The girls' trousers darkened at the hems where they trailed along the ground blotting up the moisture. In the distance she caught sight of the headlights. As the procession neared she saw a grey-suited man walking in front of the white limousine, followed by two pink stretch limousines, their windows black, unable to see the white grief-stricken faces. The pupils were amazing; not one coughed or sneezed or fidgeted. As the cortège drew close, the silence was even more silent. Eyes quietly filled with tears

They had been married thirty-five years. A lifetime. To her it didn't seem that long, but it was before there were tea bags. She remembered using leaf tea and for many years didn't have a strainer. There was always half an inch of tea left in the bottom of the cup. And she used cups, cups and saucers. She used to serve half a grapefruit for breakfast and brought it to life with a glacé cherry in the middle, even though her husband couldn't stand cherries. She scrubbed her "new" husband's Levis with a floor brush, a leg at a time, on the draining board. They would hang on the line, dripping for days, and dry like cardboard. Televisions were black and white; not that they had one, but if they had, it would have been. They had a record player and when her husband was on the late shift she used to play music and dance on her own to Rod Stewart in the big empty sitting room. Compared with now, it was another time. She thought she was just the same; she certainly felt energetic. Her hair was a similar length and a similar colour. But her face was thinner. It had lost its youthful plumpness. The once firm skin had begun to slacken. Lines appeared etched around her eyes and across her forehead. On Thursday her eldest son had bought a *Daily Mail*. It lay folded in half on the floor. She had picked it up and opened it, rapidly turning the pages until something caught her eye. She found yoga exercises for the face. She tore it out and put it in the kitchen drawer, along with all the other things she planned to read when she had time. She promised herself she would do the exercises when no one was looking, lying in the dark or sitting in a queue of traffic. Of course she had changed.

For all that time, they had lived in the same small town. Nearly everything about it had changed in that time. She had grown with the changes. At the time she had barely noticed, and it wasn't until she looked back and thought about it that she realized. She walked into town. The sun was warm on her face. People sat alfresco at The Picture House Café. Continental-style chrome tables and chairs spilled across the pavement, the smell of bacon drifted invitingly. It was situated at the end of the row of shops that struggled to survive in the uneconomic climate. Excitedly they would open up, and within a year they would stand empty, with a "To Let" flier pasted across the window. The Arcade, as it was known, used to be a cinema called The Electra. She remembered going.

In an effort to modernize, all the old uneven footpaths had been replaced with smart new block paving. Kerbs had been lowered and the roads raised. The traffic lights in the centre of town had long gone and had been replaced with a mini-roundabout. She went to the library to get a book about Brazil. That too had changed. There were computers where people could access the internet and DVDs and videos and magazines for people to borrow and newspapers to read on comfy chairs. There were a few books. Most of the useful shops in the High Street had gone and had been replaced with charity shops and estate agents and places to eat. Some shops had moved. Boots had moved three times, ultimately to save money or make more. She remembered the second Boots; standing with her youngest son waiting to be served when a madman came in. He swept his arm across the perfume shelves, scattering all the little bottles that crashed to the floor. There was devastation; shards of glass glistened in puddles of perfume. The smell was pungent and heavy. Customers and assistants alike stared in disbelief as the shop lay in chaos. The Post Office too had moved, for the same reasons. Her husband was always reminding her that they used to have a gas showroom, an electric showroom, two television shops, hardware shops, a coal office and independent shops where you could buy things. There was even a shop called Cooper's that sold tractors on Market Hill. Nowadays she could cycle into town, do her shopping and be home before the potatoes had come to the boil.

Before the days of owning a washing machine, she used to go to the launderette, just down from the café, and sit and read the paper in the smoke-filled atmosphere while her washing churned. Now it was a kitchen and bathroom shop. The things that had remained the same were the church, The Swan Revived Hotel and the most of the pubs. With the recent smoking ban in place the local brewer had updated and decorated all its premises around the town, stripping out the nicotine-coloured flocked wallpaper and stained carpets and replacing the dated furniture. Not before time, she thought.

The fifties-style swimming pool had changed. She remembered it as an outdoor pool, opening from May until September. There was a tiered paddling pool with a fountain for the children. It was where she and her children had learned to swim. There had been a diving board and a slide and it was fun. Health and safety, what health and safety? About fifteen years ago the pool was covered to make it more cost effective and make more use of the amenity. In spite of the much newer facilities, it occurred to her as she swam how restricted and controlled the children were. They were allowed a ball. Most made a lot of noise. Two lifeguards were on duty, scanning the frothing water. One, she knew. She had taught him, or rather tried to teach him eight years ago. He had been an absolute sod, especially in RE. She told him so. He regretted it now, of course, and wished he had used his time at school more effectively. He told her that when he saw a naughty child in a swimming lesson it really annoyed him. He admitted that was how he remembered himself. She knew that he felt ashamed. It was his way of saying 'sorry, Miss.' He still called her Miss.

Livi had been on report last week and at the beginning of each lesson had to hand the pale green piece of paper to the teacher, so that effort and attitude could be assessed. Until Friday afternoon she had had a reasonable day. Then, in her lesson it all gone pear-shaped. Livi's greasy smears which had been spread across the glass panels of the door were there to remind her on Monday morning as she walked into her room. Why did she do that?

She nursed a cup of tea, her eyes lingering over the frozen garden. In the distance she could hear the hum of the motorway. The air was still. Nothing moved, not even the lightness of the bamboo leaves. The fog hung and clung to the trees, the end of the garden barely visible. Suddenly, the sparrows got up and started twittering, breaking the cold metal spell. The reason that she had time to dawdle was that she had a 'work experience' appointment at nine thirty. She had been to two the day before. Alas, the employers were all of the same opinion. They, the pupils, lacked motivation. They did not communicate. They were tired and they were bored. In spite of their bravado in school, their legs ached, they hid under the counter, sat on the back stairs and cried in the toilet. They loafed around with their hands in their pockets. They simply could not be bothered. "It's been like pulling teeth," said one employer. "Like watching paint dry," said another. Wake up to the real world, she thought. It did not surprise her. That was how they were in school: lethargic and apathetic, uninterested, only there because they had to be, not because they wanted to be. They walked irritatingly slowly from lesson to lesson. No wonder they were getting fat. They would rather be wired up to their iPods and texting furiously on their latest phone. That was what life was about. No wonder they couldn't communicate.

She remembered being a Saturday girl at Antoinette's, a hairdresser's overlooking the High Street, where she used to live. She spent her day being useful. She handed end papers and pins to the stylists. She swept up hair with a soft broom, guiding the broom round the legs of the white and gold furniture. In the winter, condensation would stream down the windows and in the summer the sash windows would be thrown up and all the doors would bang shut in the draught. In her half-hour lunch break she would spend 2s. 11d. on stockings in Dorothy Perkins and buy a Ski hazelnut yoghurt. The "girls" used to clean their engagement rings in alcohol. The lady who owned the salon was not poor and lived in a big house in a nearby village. She could afford contact lenses, expensive in those days, and one day she dropped one on the floor. Everyone was on their hands and knees looking for it. Bleached hair felt brittle in her hands and although it lathered well, rinsing it was not so easy. The bubbles got caught up in the dry, matted tangle and needed severe amounts of conditioner and patient combing to free the knots. She invited the customer to "come through" after wrapping their wet hair in a towel. She would pull out a spindly white chair for the customer, making sure she was comfortable, then remove the towel and wrap a new one around her shoulders, looking in the mirror and talking to her as she did so, reassuring her. If it was long, time-consuming hair she would be asked to comb it through. She watched the stylist section the hair and deftly wind the hair round the rollers, flicking stray ends in with a tail comb. Once the hair was set, she would loosely tie it in a net and pop a cotton wool ball over each ear. "Would you like to come through?" she would say, taking the customer through to the dryer. Carefully she lowered the hood of the dryer and handed the customer the control switch and a magazine. Twenty minutes later, returning to the customer, her complexion would be florid and her pink scalp taut and shiny between the rollers. She invited her back to the spindly white chair to remove the pins and the rollers ready for the stylist to brush through. Even though it was poorly paid and her hands bled, she looked forward to her Saturday job. It was a flavour of being grown up, not a child, not a daughter, but independent. She was just fourteen, younger than the pupils she was visiting. Visiting the work placements gave her the chance of seeing behind the High Street façade, the warren of corridors and offices piled high with box files, never to be opened. She remembered the baker's being a double-fronted shop, a ladies' dress outfitter's called Vera's. The florist had, in the past, been a fruit and vegetable shop, selling underrated, overpriced produce. How they sold anything was beyond her. The chemist had been a Salvation Army charity shop and a bargain store and Boots, where the man had lost his cool. She was curious about these private worlds and could now picture how it was behind the frontage. The bucket of flowers wedging the door open, the Celebration chocolates scattered across the table and the toilet where the boy had cried.

Back on January 11th, when she had had her new group, she said "Just because it's Friday afternoon, I expect the lessons to be as good as the first lesson on Monday morning." That was hard to live up to, not only for the pupils, but for her as well. She had a spring in her step on Friday afternoon and found herself glancing at the clock. The pupils couldn't wait for three thirty either. Fortunately, Livi kept her head down, but that she found disconcerting. She wouldn't put anything past her. There were four boys, two black and two white, and all they wanted to do was sing and rap. They kept their eye on her and as soon as her back was turned they would stand in a line practising the steps. Well, it was harmless – at least they were not throwing vegetables at each other. "Let's dance," she said to Mandy as she emptied peelings into the bin by the window. "Look! Miss and Mrs Simmons are dancing," the boys shrieked. Everyone laughed and carried on with the washing up. After all, it was Friday afternoon.

Seconds earlier or later and she would have missed the vibrant spectacle in all its brilliance. Recognizing the unmistakable trilling whistle made her stop and turn. The dazzling turquoise iridescence flew fast and straight, low over the water. It was like a precious jewel, vivid against the winter drabness, the decaying reeds bent and folded, trailing loosely in the current. Without sounding whimsical or insincere, surely no words could describe the thrill that exquisite little bird gave her. It left her feeling privileged. Some people had never seen a kingfisher. Her husband saw them all the time and took them for granted. Lucky him, she thought.

Her friend sat against the wall, which, thirty years ago had been shelves from the floor to the ceiling displaying expensive brand names of tinned fruit and vegetables, soups and milk puddings. On the opposite wall had been the counter where the money changed hands, where bacon was cut to size on a big red slicing machine and where pink and white sugared mice sat alongside the shoelaces, the Omo and the Vim. Halyards the Purveyors had been a truly original independent grocery store. She had known her good friend since they had pushed their babies in buggies. She had seemed troubled the day before when she had seen her out walking her dogs. She lived in the same house as her husband and that was as good as it got. She always thought her friend was wasted, working in Marks and Spencers. She was clever and creative and had gone to university. She knew the Latin names of plants and could identify all the different ducks on the river. She was good at learning and remembered everything. Two years ago she "retired" and retrained in social care and now worked in a local school in the SEN department. Still wasted. She was seriously analytical about different issues and hilariously funny about others. She had phoned her friend in the morning, before she had time to think about her day. "Let's go for lunch." And they did. "Prego" had survived a couple of years. The restaurant had taken over the very dilapidated shop and transformed it. The fresh blue and tiled floor captured a trendy Mediterranean atmosphere. Stepping in, it did not feel quite as she expected it to. It did not, in her opinion feel Italian enough. The food was fine but the conversation better. The red wine warmed and the espresso sharpened. They hugged on the corner where Bury Street met Silver Street and said goodbye. She walked home, pleased, her back to the cold icy wind.

Scanning their work for mistakes, she wondered how many times she had written "equipment" and "safty" in red biro. At least half the class had written "equitment" and "safety". She remembered clearly saying "equip'ment", emphasising the "p", not "equit-ment". And it was "safe-ty". Do they listen? Do they heck.

The early daffodils lay sprawled across the grass, unable to lift their yellow heads. It was a good enough reason to do some spring-cleaning. Housework is a noun and means the work of running a home, such as cleaning, cooking and shopping. She didn't do much of the first one. Launching into housework was done only when it was absolutely essential, if visitors were staying, for instance. Each week she vacuumed and dusted and cleaned the bathroom, but that was only the tip of the iceberg. Making a start in her bedroom, she noticed on the carpet, creamy-coloured empty cocoons of a moth or a beetle, like miniature husks from an ear of wheat. Once she had pushed and shoved the furniture away from the wall she noticed the threadbare carpet in the corner. Something had an appetite for carpet. On her hands and knees she vacuumed with the short narrow attachment on full power, sucking in dust and skin particles. Then she proceeded to wash the skirting board. Then, with the soft brush attachment, she vacuumed the walls and the backs of the furniture. When did she last do this? Had she ever done this? When everything was back in place, she lovingly cleaned the surfaces with lavender polish. Those gastronomic carpet eaters had probably long gone and were quietly enjoying a meal somewhere else, in another corner of the house, well away from cloths wrung out in Ocean Breeze and frightening sucking pipes that lifted them and their dinner off the floor.

"I'll check the parcel that came this morning. What is the name please?" The assistant turned and went into the small office at the end of the shop. "It's here," she said, reappearing holding a small buff-coloured envelope. She slipped the necklace onto the scroll of velvet on the counter and arranged it for her to admire. It looked beautiful. It had been broken for years. The string at the clasp had rotted with the sweat from her neck and the warmth of her hair at the nape of her neck. She had felt it slip off her neck and in one swift movement had caught it. The necklace had been in a bag at the back of her drawer ever since. Everything about the necklace was written on the buff envelope: the number of beads, graduating in size, the colour, the red string and the knots in between and her name and the receipt number. Her husband had bought her the necklace in Venice twenty years ago. There had been too many lovely necklaces to choose from. In the end she chose the red glass beads; they were heavy and felt good in her hand, like a bag of marbles. She remembered that hot Wednesday afternoon. It had been part of a round trip, but the highlight and main intention of going was to see Venice in case the opportunity never arose again. The coach left Lake Bled, in Slovenia, very early in the morning and on the way visited the amazing caves in Postojna and the famous Lippizaner horses – typical tourist attractions – and stopped for lunch for the most unedible bowl of thin, transparent soup. It was watery grey with pearl barley and bits of anaemic gristly animal tissue floating in it. She tried coaxing her children to eat it, returning the hospitality, not wanting to seem ungrateful and leave food, especially prepared. The children shuddered. She had to agree, it was truly disgusting. To show willing, they picked at the bread.

Venice lived up to her expectations. They visited the sights and went to a local glass factory and watched the man blowing the molten glass. Inside, his workshop was hot and dark, which made the visual effect of the demonstration even more powerful. They walked the entire length from Piazza San Marco to the gardens at the end of the Bacino di San Marco. Cruise ships moored and gondolas bobbed on the sparkling sea. On the way back, they stopped for a glass of orange, the most expensive glass of orange ever when they converted the lire back to pounds. It was her first glimpse of Italy, the faded peeling buildings, washing hanging over the watery streets, the quiet reverence of the local people sitting in the dark shade oblivious to the hordes of tourists being escorted by guides, their umbrellas leading the way.

Unlike last week's film, "Definitely Maybe", listed as a rom-com, this week's film was of epic proportions.

First of all, she wondered when the film "There Will Be Blood", was going to get going and then she wondered when it was going to end. She had parked the car for four hours assuming that to be enough time. By four fifteen, her time was dangerously running out. It made her fidgety and she kept tilting her wrist to see if she could make out the time in the dark. She was becoming anxious, more about the real life drama than the one she had paid to see. The bargain Tuesday film would not be much of a bargain if she had to pay a parking fine. She almost ran to her car, relieved not to see a ticket on the screen or the inspector hovering.

She sat at the kitchen table talking to her son. They made endless cups of tea, sometimes in the teapot, sometimes in the cup. Over the years the shape of the table had changed but he always sat in 'his' place, facing the window. Every now and then he would check the fridge, hoping to see something interesting to eat. Sometimes, when he called, she made a coffee with boiled milk. She saw it as a good way of using up the milk and making sure that she wasn't calcium deficient. It irritated her that the very same thing was called a latte. Surely that just meant milk in Italian, but sounded much more enticing, like foreign words did, adopted and used as though they were ours, like mange-tout and fromage. She liked talking to Joe. He was interesting and lively, always a different project on the go. Sometimes they fell silent and that was all right too.

They met at The Old Red Lion on Kennington Park Road, opposite Kennington underground station. She squeezed her son and kissed him on the cheek. His face was cold and he smelled of the fresh air, if you could call London air, fresh. Another round was ordered. It was good to see him. She had gone on the train with her husband to meet up with two of their sons and have a meal. Her husband wanted to sit by the window so that he could see the stretch of the canal that he was so familiar with. He had picked up a leaflet about attractions in London and proceeded to go through it, pointing out things that might interest her. They were not going to any of the attractions listed, it was just a way of passing the time. It was an effortless journey and they were early. They turned right at the entrance of the underground. It was familiar to her husband. He remembered it from last year when he had gone to the Oval to watch the cricket with his son. They crossed the busy road to the pub. Although there were three doors, it didn't look open. Gently, she pushed the middle door. The light was gloomy. People sat at the bar. An older man sat at a table on his own, with his stereo for company and a half-empty pint glass. She and her husband sat on the tall stools at the bar and ordered a pint of beer, a glass of red wine and a bag of cheese-and-onion crisps. A man was talking to his mate about something in a cardboard box that was on a nearby table. The man had his children with him and they also sat at the bar sucking lemonade through straws, laughing when the bubbling, gurgling sound indicated that the lemonade was finished. The three of them turned into Braganza Street and zig-zagged through the housing estate and across the park to Cadiz Street. She remembered driving her son with all his stuff to the terraced house that he shared with three other student friends. It was clean and comfortable. Her husband was shown around. He kept shaking his head, reminiscing as he was prone to do. He greatly admired his son for what he had done and what he had achieved. Leaving him standing at the bus-stop, outside the V&A, turning round as the bus pulled away, waving goodbye At the time he was close to tears. "And now look at him. Four years later, confident and self-assured." He rubbed his hand across his bony shoulders and squeezed his arm around him. Proud. Once the house in Cadiz Street had been viewed, the three of them made their way back to the tube station bound for Goodge Street. A call of nature sent them diving into the nearest pub, although they didn't need excuses. Looking out, she saw Alex. It was his posture, walking at a hundred miles an hour, head down. Guy called him on his phone and told him to stop and turn round. Moments later he was there, peeling off his jacket and pulling off his grey woolly hat. It was drinks all round and they settled into a warm, relaxed contentment. It had rained, the street was shiny and lights stretched out, reflected. Tyres hissed in the wet. They crossed the road to the restaurant. She had been to Zizzi many times with her children, so many times that a silly family quip "it'z ezzi at Zizzi" had rolled off the tongue and always caused a smile. For her, it was easy.

Billed as 'ARE YOU EXPERIENCED?', she was keen to see if a tribute band could compare to the real thing. John Campbell was undoubtedly talented and had tremendous admiration for the original band. Flawless, frenzied, frantic guitar playing, notes piled on top of each other, confused and blurred into another sound, echoing the one and only intense schizophrenic energy of Jimi Hendrix. His hands lithe, his teeth and fingers nimble, effortlessly clever over the guitar strings, culminating with the mad burning of a perfectly good guitar, while singing 'Wild Thing'. She doubted that any of the band members had seen the legendary Jimi Hendrix live, as she had done forty years ago. They were too young. In spite of their high-octane energy and amazing sound, her disappointment was with their appearance, especially "Jimi's". Sadly, his clothes were not flamboyant, and although he had the right type of hair, he didn't have enough of it. He wasn't tall enough or thin enough. His trousers weren't tight enough, nor were they hipsters in crushed purple velvet that flared out over Cuban heeled boots. He should have worn his lace shirt unbuttoned, open to the waist. At the interval he changed into comfortable jersey exercise trousers with white moccasins. He definitely lacked the voodoo magic and purple haze. Equalizing did not reduce the whirring noise in her head. Thankfully, when she woke the next morning, the sound of a million insects had finally gone.

The precious last day of the holiday and she had a lunchtime birthday party to go to. Jeans were requested and absolutely no presents. Phoning to confirm, she asked if she could bring a bottle of wine or some flowers. No, absolutely no presents, was the reply, reiterating the note on the invitation. The plan was that each guest was to pledge two hours of their time to visit the friend in question, in the next year. For many that would be a tall order. She could see why jeans were requested. The relaxed easy atmosphere changed when the hired mini bus turned left. Chris was a keen gardener and enjoyed plants and wildlife. The seven birthday guests had put forward a number of theories for the dress code: a garden makeover, a walk, a visit to the museum of rural life. No one had guessed the venue. None of them had ever been karting before. Conversation practically ceased. They lost their bubbling confidence. The women became anxious and unsure. They had to put their details on the computer and sign in. They were asked to sign the printout and were then given a black and red quilted all-in-one suit, along with gloves and a hairnet, then directed to the communal changing rooms. Once the belongings were safely installed in the lockers, which were difficult to master, it was time to watch the safety video. She would have been more than happy spending the afternoon in Chris's front room. The all-important helmets were fitted and everyone went outside, the Rocky music blaring. Her helmet was a snug fit. It was too snug. Her hair she scooped into the hairnet. Her hairband pressed into her head and, somehow, her ears had got folded and she could feel her amber earrings digging in. The protective foam inside the helmet clenched her cheeks and she looked like a surprised hamster. The tense apprehension was evident as they waited by their cars in the pit stop. She was hesitant in the practice lap, not sure that she could overtake, being polite, letting others pass, gripping the wheel tightly, pressing the brake, concentrating. After the practice heat the women pulled into the pit stop and deliberated. Each received a lap time analysis sheet of their performance. In heat two, their lack of confidence changed. Suddenly the women were wickedly competitive, overtaking wildly, aggressively cutting corners and hitting the barriers. By heat three, fearless determination broke all records. Their insecurity had been shattered. Back in the safety of Chris's front room the glass of red wine was much needed and well deserved. Returning home, she could tell her husband wasn't interested in her afternoon. He wasn't interested in her best lap time. He wasn't listening to her. He was more interested in the football match on the television and when he was going to get something to eat. She felt hurt. Until then, it had been a good day.

She turned to the cinema listings in the free newspaper to check showing times. There on the page was a picture of Jack Nicholson and Morgan Freeman, and, although it was blurred, it was Cairo in the background. She recognized the view, the pink hazy polluted air hanging over the city's skyline. East meeting west. Even though it was a black-and-white photo she knew the haze would be pink and she knew the minarets would be gold. She could hear the call to prayer in her head. Along with other places and other dreams, visiting Cairo had been on Edward's and Carter's "Bucket List". She liked to think that she had an ongoing bucket list and was determined that nothing should pass her by, not leaving it to the last minute when she couldn't live life to the full. Simple everyday things like making a perfect poached egg or seeing a carpet of bluebells or hearing a babbling brook or the feel of silk. They were just as important as seeing the temples in Luxor or the blue roofs on the island of Thira or New York skyscrapers, or feeling the warm sticky waters of the Blue Lagoon or being in Djemaa el fna at sunset, feeling the tension, the pulsating expectation of the night ahead or diving in the Red Sea. She didn't sit watching the film thinking, I must go there or I must do that. She had already had a taste of other worlds. "A man of words and not of deeds is like a garden full of weeds". She was a woman of deeds.

March

The earthquake measured 5.3 on the Richter Scale. At the time she hadn't known that it was an earthquake. At the time she couldn't explain the trembling sensation, preceded by what she thought was a flock of birds, biggish birds landing on the roof above her head, blown off course on their way to spring breeding grounds. Then the bed began to shake violently. It was a big solid bed, which, only the other day, she could barely move in her spring-cleaning frenzy. In addition, she and her husband lay blissfully asleep, their combined weight approximately twenty stones, anchoring the bed permanently. Immediately she got up and pulled her dressing gown around her and wandered around the house. She opened the curtains and looked out over the road and saw nothing unusual. Shaking and fluttering, she went back to bed. The earthquake was not the first item when she turned the radio on to catch the six o'clock news. It should have been. It hadn't been a flock of birds after all, it had been the tiles jiggling before the tremor. In the evening, two scientists explained the shifting plates and concocted a cardboard model to demonstrate what had happened the previous night.

All week she had been chipping away at the marking – one hundred and seventy projects in total, each needing a short paragraph, a mark out of ten and a national curriculum level. She marked them all, sitting askew on the settee, leaning on the world atlas. She was never short of entertainment. There were oven "glothes" for "gloves"; "I must try my beast" "My 'behavior' is 'exerlent'"; "noing" instead of "knowing"; and "flower" instead of "flour". She wrote "ww" beside "flower", indicating "wrong word". It was exciting stuff. No, she must not use the word "stuff": it was a "couldn't be bothered" word that she frequently crossed out when used in place of a noun. For example, "to grate cheese" they would write, "to grate stuff" or even "to great stuff". Then she would write "ww" beside "great" indicating "wrong word". On top of that, on Thursday it was parents' evening. She saw that as a public relations exercise, chatting to parents, trying to tell them nicely what little shits their children actually were. Sometimes it placed the children sitting beside their parents in the most intolerable position, their parents quizzing them on why the homework wasn't done in front of their teacher. Not very cool.

On Thursday night she was wakeful. It must have been the late evening at school. Also, she wanted to talk about packaging materials to her year eleven group and had planned to do her shopping before school so that it could be used as a resource. Logistically it was a big job, but it would be worth it. Thinking about it kept her awake. She found a shopping trolley in the service corridor at school and used it in her demonstration. She wheeled her shopping to the front of the class and proceeded to lift out the "bags for life". The class wondered where she had obtained the trolley. She said that she had found it under one of the many bridges spanning the dual carriageways. "What, you found it and put it in your car?"

"Yes," she lied. Well, she couldn't back down now. The lesson didn't have the wow factor that she had hoped for. The class, mainly the girls, were more interested in going out on Friday night. On Friday afternoon, Darren and Tom explained what was meant by the "beats". "It is the African culture, Miss."

44

She made sure that Darren had a new homework book. "Just as well I didn't say anything else to your mum," she said. Thankfully, Livi was absent.

All weekend, apart from her hour swimming on Sunday morning, she had spent marking. The immense effort to complete those bloody projects had left her drained, her energy stores depleted. It had left her feeling tired and pissed off, unable to cope with the demands of year nine on Monday morning. She started calmly, demonstrating how a Swiss roll should be made, sharing her expertise. It didn't last long. Seeing two girls sieving their flour into a half-whisked mixture, she was so cross she banged her hand on the worktop, insisting that all ten whisks were brought to a stop. "You need to whisk for five minutes, maybe six." Whisking resumed. The girls in year eleven continued where they had left off on Friday morning. She blamed the media, the round-the-clock, wall-to-wall entertainment, the never-ending, screaming in-your-face sensationalism, glamorous and glitzy, everything all hyped up, beyond all sense of proportion, out of reach. Her husband blamed the "Tories". She liked to think that she could make a difference. She liked to think that she would leave the children that she taught with a lasting impression and when they finally fell silent and accepted what she was showing them she knew that they would not forget. It could be something as simple as rolling up a Swiss roll or dragging a cocktail stick through coloured icing to create a feathery pattern on a biscuit, when they couldn't work out how something was going to be done and they wanted to know.

"What do you think, Miss? My mum said that I should concentrate on my exams, but I want to go out with my boyfriend. I'm sixteen next month." Implying that she was old enough to decide.

"Well, Carrie," she replied. "I started going out with my boyfriend when I was just fifteen and have been with him for forty-two years." Basically, things hadn't changed. She didn't discourage the boyfriend and she didn't side with the mother either. It was for Carrie to make her own decision.

True to her word, Darren's mother stood over him holding the birch. Darren was proud to hand her his completed homework booklet. She sighed. Not more marking.

As always, she looked forward to going home. In the evening she made pasties and a date-and-walnut cake.

She stood beside the table. The children were watching her hands manoeuvring the tailoring shears, slicing effortlessly along the dangerously narrow white line between the photographs.

"Why do you use such big scissors, Miss?"

"They are called shears not scissors," she replied. "I use them because they are comfortable and easy to hold and the blades are long so they are more accurate."

She liked cutting up the sheet of photographs. She liked having to be precise, the slightest error rendering the photos useless and the delay of having to get them reprinted, irritating. She would be annoyed with herself. She was the same when she had top-stitched the edge of a collar in the days when she used the shears for their correct purpose. She told the children that she used to use them for textiles. "What are textiles, Miss?"

"You know, fabrics, materials. Like your shirt."

"Like your fluffy jumper Miss."

She hadn't dared to wear the soft angora jumper in their lesson since one of the boys couldn't resist stroking her arm as though she was a cat. They pictured a grubby outworker, piles of dull bodice fronts and bodice backs being machined at the shoulders.

"No." she replied, "I used to teach textiles and before that I used to be a designer."

"Were you not a chef, Miss?"

"No, I have never been a chef."

In less than an hour she would be quietly pressing Maltesers against the roof of her mouth, the chocolate dissolving, coating her teeth, her tongue revisiting bits of honeycomb wedged between. The light airy temptations were a treat from her friend, who insisted that they each had a packet. Screen Ten was showing "The Bank Job". It reminded her of how London used to be. It was a coincidence that only last week she heard the theme tune for "Take Three Girls" and she had sung along with it. Her husband didn't remember the weekly series on Thursday evenings. But she remembered watching it on the rented black-and-white television in the sitting room, her mother feeling uncomfortable when it came on. She would wince and fidget in her chair. She thought it was risqué and didn't like her daughter being corrupted. London in those days was so removed from the village she had lived in and she was extremely interested in finding out what it was like. The film brought it back. She remembered going to the Portobello Road as a student and investing in a real fur coat, with hard padded shoulders, and wearing it hippie style with her hair long. She remembered going to Biba in Kensington High Street, with its atmospheric mood, rails and rails of clothes, mini skirts and maxi coats in dusty colours, pallets of matching make-up, feather boas, suede knee-high boots and carpet bags. She remembered the dilapidation around Earls Court, and the seedy Soho streets portrayed in the film, where her mother would have forbidden her to go. It was exciting and exhilarating and, anyway, her mother never knew.

The Swiss rolls were impressive. It was hard to choose three over and above the others. After much deliberation she chose David's Swiss roll as one. It had all the criteria that she expected to see in a good quality product. It had an even colour, it was neatly rolled up, it hadn't cracked on the edges and it was a good sponge. "How on earth have you managed to earn a merit? I can't believe that you of all people have made such a good Swiss roll," she laughed. He smiled, his cheeks sunned and golden after his snowboarding adventures at half term. She was always on his case. He was messy, disorganized, slap-dash and impatient. Even that morning he had had the electric whisk full on, waving it around when he should have been washing his hands. She had not shared the easy banter with David's sister; he was so different from her.

She woke during the night with a headache. It had been trying to make an appearance the previous day but had never quite made it. Unsettled, she lay there, hoping sleep would cure it. She knew that it was probably because she had become dehydrated rushing around, not stopping all day. Eventually, she got up and had a glass of warm water and two paracetamol. She lay, curled on the settee, willing the wretched feeling to go away. All too soon it was time to get ready for school. There had been an upset. Tom's big black eyes were filled with tears. He made his shepherd's pie. It transpired that he wasn't going to Darren's birthday party. Not until the evening did the headache finally clear.

It was a bright sunny morning as she pulled into the car park. A man in a fluorescent "high-vis" jacket waved her across the rough car park and into a parking place. The Bowl was a local outdoor arena for rock concerts, but on Sunday mornings it hosted the weekly car boot sale. The sweet sickly smell of doughnuts hung in the air near the gate. The wide path around The Bowl was lined with stalls, selling all and sundry, second-hand goods, new goods at bargain prices, and stolen goods all laid out on rickety pasting tables, garden furniture, unrolled carpets and plastic sheeting, that lifted and flapped when the wind got underneath it. Van doors were open and car boots were up. She was there because she was looking for stolen goods, goods that two days before had belonged to her son, stolen from his locked alarmed car. There were tools, but some were too old to be Joe's and some too new, still in their hard vacuum-formed packaging. She looked methodically, scanning backwards and forwards, peering into cardboard boxes, searching with her eyes. She would have recognized them if they had been there. Trading in this way, out in the open, cash only, appealed. It was heaving with local people, immigrants, housed nearby. It was these people that were said to be upsetting the indigenous people. There were Indians and Africans and white people from Eastern Europe trying to make things better for themselves, their voices foreign. The women from Eastern Europe looked hard and brassy, pushing their babies in flimsy buggies, cigarettes pressed to their lips, dressed in tightly zipped denim and high-heeled shoes. There were dogs: every type of designer dog, walking to heel beside their owners, waiting patiently while they browsed. People stood still and lit cigarettes in cupped hands. They smoked openly in a public space and thought nothing of it. There seemed to be no rules, no laws, no CCTV cameras to keep an eye, so removed from the big glossy shopping centre with its flagship stores just down the road.

The threat of the forthcoming storms filled the airwaves. At every opportunity forecasters warned of the severe weather that was going to sweep east across southern England, leaving a trail of destruction. True enough, gale-force winds brought trees and power lines down. Some roads were closed because of the strength of the wind and there was disruption to rail services and flights. Rivers were brown and full, swollen with the heavy driving rain, in a hurry to get to the sea. Like black rags, crows tried flying. Gulls took the easy option and gathered on the playing field.

Her year nine group were true to form. The innocence of the feather icing lesson was lost on them. She could not compete with their anti-social behaviour. Chaos ensued when they started making the piping bag. She knew it would. Distracted by each other, they hadn't watched her demonstration. She had showed the paper-folding three times, but of course they already knew what to do. Why did they need a demonstration?

"Put the folded edge towards your tummy. Put your finger opposite the point. Take the left side up, turn it in to form a cone. Pick it up, wrap it round, line it up and roll it down." It was far too complicated for them on a Monday morning. How, in all the confusion, had she managed to catch the psychedelic kaleidoscope, a spotlight of colour, brilliant and bleeding? The effect was accidental, a vivid, intense surprise, colours applied directly, not as she had shown. Until he messed it up and ate it, Stefan's biscuit was amazing. Well, it didn't improve. The lesson was endured until lunchtime, when she opened the gate of the pen and let the animals out to play. Why did she bother with the likes of them, intent on spoiling and ruining her lesson? Maybe it was the wind. She always blamed the wind when the children were particularly uncontrollable.

Emerging from the cinema complex on Tuesday evening, the wind had increased again and whipped her hair round her face, stinging her cheeks. She bent into the ripping, snatching cyclone and, hugging her coat tightly, ran to the car. Relieved, she closed the door. Safe. Thinking about the film on the way home she thought that Juno was too cosy, too perfect. Juno was smart,

49

American smart. A precocious schoolgirl, irritatingly cool, so self-assured and in control. Where was the turmoil? Where was the anger? Where were the shock and the raised voices when Juno told her parents she was pregnant? They didn't flinch, they completely understood. Confidently, the conceited Juno explained that she was going to give her baby to Mark and Vanessa who had advertised in the 'wanted ads' for a baby. Brave and good, she had got it all planned out. Bleeker, the still-wet-behind-the-ears father, didn't get a look in. The nine-month gestation was a piece of cake. After that time Juno resumed her life as though nothing had happened. It simply wasn't like that. Her face was perfect too.

Rob opened a drawer in his work area. There was Tom's shepherd's pie with a furry grey mould on top.

Fair Trade was the topic on Friday morning and by 6.30 a.m. Fair Trade products were flying off the supermarket shelves. She wanted the pupils to understand that it meant a better quality of life for Fatima Lopez in Nicaragua and Erica Kyere in Ghana. She passed round some chocolate to taste, made from Mrs Kyere's cocoa beans and made a pot of coffee with Mrs Lopez's fresh-ground coffee. The pupils were interested in the cafetière and wanted to know how to use it. She explained the word "ambience" and that the fresh coffee smell helps to create an easy, relaxed atmosphere. She liked arousing their senses, exposing them to culinary experiences. Some were not fortunate enough to have smelled fresh coffee or tasted a passion fruit. In her youth, she would have been one of those and knew what it felt like not to know. At lunchtime she sat with Mandy having a cup of tea and a Jazzy apple, cored and cut into slices. They talked about coffee pots and the thin spiders that lived in the kitchen cupboards too high to use on a regular basis without getting the stepladder from the garage. In her cupboard above the pots and pans were the plastic lolly moulds, play dough cutters and plywood farm animal stencils left over from when her children were small, when they would spend a lot of their time playing in the kitchen at the table or on the floor. She talked about her Denby stoneware dishes that proved so difficult to break and were now distributed between her children and how, only the other day, she had seen a coffee set, the very same design, in Oxfam for ten pounds. She pictured it in the shelf, the cups taller than her teacups with saucers. It had been worth ten pounds. She should have bought it. She had said to a boy the other day to get a saucer from the cupboard. He had no idea what a saucer was. She told Mandy how she had first seen the half-pint casserole dish and loved its neat chunky shape. It was the start of collecting.

She stood all the way, not once seeing the view that she knew so well. All she could see were the lines, merging and separating, merging and separating, converging and emerging, tunnels black, the track widening and narrowing, hypnotizing and mesmerizing for the entire journey. The train did not stop. Usually she took an interest in the passengers, how they were dressed or what they were reading. Today she didn't. Immediately to her left two girls shared a bottle of designer juice, arranging plastic cups on the fold-down table. They chatted away and seemed to be awash with plastic carrier bags. As the train pulled in they began to talk to two girls opposite, in Welsh. Due to maintenance work, she slightly diverted her route and went via Kings Cross then on the Circle line to High Street Kensington. Originally, it had been her intention to go to Portobello Road to reminisce and by mistake she got off the tube at Notting Hill Gate. As soon as she stepped off, she knew she wasn't where she wanted to be. She walked down Church Street past the antique shops. Three times she stopped to look in windows. She saw a pair of weathered stone kestrels perched on an old chair for £320 and saw the sharpest bed linen, crisp and white, trimmed in blue, making her own seem uncomfortably shoddy, and then she stopped to look in the patisserie to admire the decorated cakes at £25. There was a good mix of shops in Kensington High Street, all within a short walk of each other. She checked them all. Looking, feeling, holding garments against her, looking in the mirror. One or two things caught her eye and many reminded her of fashion in the late sixties and although she wore them then, forty years later she found them too youthful. She knew she was difficult to please and didn't buy anything. She made her way to the underground to meet up with two of her sons and a girlfriend at Leicester Square. They ate in Med Kitchen at Cambridge Circus. Disappointingly, even at 2 p.m., Alex was hung over and couldn't make it for lunch but would make it for 5 p.m. at the British Museum. Guy announced that because there were only three of them they could indulge and have all three courses. Between them they shared antipasti. The carnivores ate the salami and the prosciutto and the herbivore ate the roasted vegetables and the rocket, followed by more roasted vegetables and chickpeas-imported ideas, while the carnivores ate duck cassoulet, finishing with raspberry brûlée – more imported ideas. They talked about pure English food and decided that their diet would be very meat-based which didn't fill the herbivore with much hope. She cracked the glassy top of the brûlée with her teaspoon. It was good. The music was random, a bit of everything, appealing to all. Their table overlooked the Circus. Aptly named, thronging with denim and grey, people going this way and that. Several times, police sirens and fire engines interrupted the silent scene. There was a music shop across the road and afterwards the three of them went in. She didn't find it difficult to choose some CDs. She was not going home empty-handed after all. The three of them walked to the British Museum along the Charing Cross Road, stopping off once to see if Foyles had got the 2008 Playfair cricket annual for her husband. No luck. It started to rain. She stood on the top step, waiting for Alex. Around her, in the darkening afternoon, cameras were flashing. Visitors, especially the Japanese, were taking photographs of each other, with the famous colonnade in the background. He could see her and they waved to each other. She ran down the steps into the rain. She squeezed her son and took his arm. She had booked the tickets a month ago to see the exhibition of The First Emperor. The terracotta army was amazing, their quiet earthy colour humbling. Until the end, it was an impressive show. What spoilt it for her was the gaudy painted figure at the end where the stairs descended straight into the shop, where the terracotta army was printed on everything. Linked sales memorabilia, often cheap and tacky, did not interest her. It was probably all made in China anyway. Dehydration had kicked in; they were in need of a drink. They made their way to the Fitzrovia in Godge Street, where they had been before. It was busy with early St Patrick's Day revellers, football fans, rugby fans and a stag night party; the man in question was actually dressed as a stag. They all hugged and kissed and said goodbye to Guy and Abbi at the underground. She walked back to Euston with Alex. The traffic hissed in the wet.

She had half an hour to wait for her train at nine o'clock. They stood under the departures board. The lightness of the day changed to emotional upheaval, quiet secrets aired. They talked about love. She said that she thought that there were different types of love and she wondered if she really knew what love was. What she did know was that she loved her children absolutely unconditionally, and she loved her husband, but not in the same way and not as she had done forty years ago when she said to him that she loved him. Did she really know what love was then? Alex wanted some guidance, something to tell him that he was doing the right thing or the wrong thing. She couldn't advise him, but she did say that he must do what felt right for him and he would know when it was right. They walked down the slope nearer the train. They hugged and hugged. Their eyes were wet with tears. She turned and watched him walk back up the slope. He did not turn round. Once again, the machine did not accept her ticket flashing on the screen "seek assistance". The train was full. People were already standing. Many had been to football matches and the rugby at Twickenham. They were reading their programmes. She stood holding the rail above her head. A male smell, a beery fast food fart, drifted upwards. She turned her head away. There were three women in the carriage. It was none of them; she could tell.

It was just the sort of day to stay in – cold, windy and rainy. The meadow was getting smaller, the muddy brown floodwaters slowly seeping, just a spit of grass visible. A day to hibernate, to drink hot chocolate and coffee and snack on biscuits. She listened to her CDs. Porcelain was the fourth track. It so reminded her of her son, not the sons she had seen yesterday. The distant menacing moody sound was haunting, another time. Losing My Religion was the track she had heard in Med Kitchen and the reason for the impromptu purchases. Knowing that she would feel useless by the end of the day if she didn't go out and face the world, she went swimming. She said hello to some, and sorry to others when she accidentally caught them with her big wide strokes. She transferred the CD from the house to the car, and back again. Like a picture in a book, the barn owl appeared silently over the hedge, light and white against the darkness.

Twice, three times including hers, she saw bad driving. She saw the girl mouthing off at her and giving her the evils at a roundabout. Normally she was proud of her driving skills and rarely stepped out of line. She knew that she had approached too fast and had to brake – hard-not an emergency stop but none the less, a firm brake. The girl in the orange Fiat was coming from the right, coming too fast. She hadn't indicated left or right. With an hour to spare, she wasn't late and neither was she in a hurry. She was listening to her new CD. The girl going straight on was in the right and she was in the wrong. Hardly two minutes later, again approaching another roundabout, she was behind a blue car in the left-hand lane when it indicated right and crossed in front of a silvery beige car. She saw the impending horror unfolding in her wing mirror. The silvery beige car stopped dead. Then at the next roundabout a girl with short blonde hair brought both lanes to a complete standstill because she had been dithery.

On Monday morning the animals returned to their pen. This week the animals made screeching monkey noises and they were in fine form. This week, one of the animals turned up the oven temperature deliberately to 220 and burnt the cakes, not once but twice.

She lay, listening to the birds chirruping and singing their hearts out at the impending dawn. If she kept her eyes open long enough she could see the light change and the shapes in her room emerge out of the darkness. In the quietness she heard the soft sound of the clock, then the harsh brittle sound of the alarm. She reached out and flicked the switch up, then withdrew her warm arm back under the covers. The silence resumed. Beside her, her husband slept on.

There were more people in the audience for the historical drama The Other Boleyn Girl than all the other films she had seen on bargain Tuesday. The adverts were blaring out as they took their seats in the dark, trying to be quiet, getting their coats off and getting comfortable, trying to open the Maltesers without a sound. They had got used to having the auditorium practically to themselves, not sharing it with about fifty women. It was undoubtedly a woman's film. All of them, including her, felt for Mary and Anne, both put in the most impossible position. Recruited by their ambitious father and uncle, the girls were encouraged to flirt for the King's attention with the possibility of bearing him a son. The film touched a nerve. Women meant nothing: there for men's convenience, their satisfaction and their gratification. Even today, women around the world were denied their right, their basic human right to have the freedom to be themselves, to be worthy of respect, not to suffer mental and physical abuse at the hands of men.

As always, her husband was flicking through the channels. It was a sordid scene. The man had his parking fine waived because he let the traffic cops feel between his girlfriend's thighs. How could the man allow the violation? How could he allow it to happen? How could he think it was OK? It was abhorrent. Deep inside her, it aroused a strange rebellious feeling, a gut instinct, to stand up and campaign for women's rights. Mrs. Smith, her elderly friend had died last summer. She had been fiercely pro women's lib, a true suffragette, who strived tirelessly for equality. She always said to her that she must use her vote. It had been a hard fight and was not yet won.

Thursday had been a day of meetings, interrupted only by break, when she went to the staff room and had a cup of tea and three digestive biscuits, and lunch, when she had vegetable lasagne and red wine in a plastic cup. They were the highlights. She didn't fare well in meetings. Basically, they were dull and boring and she seemed to achieve very little. Even by nine fifteen her eyelids were closing and the day had just begun. Sitting in meetings annoyed her so much that when she did contribute she became argumentative and flippant. She was so glad to escape at the end of the day. The phone was ringing as she unloaded the weekly shop in the hall. It was her son. He was in a terrible state. He sounded delirious, she could barely understand what he was saying. His voice was trembling and broken. He had collapsed at the station, exhausted. A kind person had given him water and some chocolate. Slowly he came back to reality. He did not want her to come into London but she insisted that she would be on the platform to help him with his luggage. Hordes of people got off the train, eager to start their Easter break. The guard was about to blow his whistle. "Excuse me," she said. "Was there a young lad with a bike? He was poorly."

"Yes" said the guard. "He will be down by the lift."

She thanked him and went off down the platform. She saw him waiting, holding his bike his backpack and his rucksack. She wriggled in to be beside him. She stood waiting for the lift, holding his hand, squeezing it gently, so glad, so relieved that he was all right. She took his bike.

During the week, it had been arranged that she and her husband were visiting friends on Friday, staying overnight and returning on Saturday morning. She was looking forward to seeing them, sitting by the fire, exhausted by its heat, alternating with tea and coffee and orange and wine, talking way past bedtime. Janet's cats curled and purring on the back of the sofa and lying in the dip between her thighs, heavy with sleep, enjoying the attention, waking every now and then to stretch out a paw and extend her claws. Even though she wasn't keen on cats, she allowed Janet's cats to do this. Usually, she found their independence unnerving. Once, when she was in a babysitting circle, sitting for her friend's daughter, Ann, she remembered Jake, a Siamese cat. He would watch her, his cold blue eyes boring into her, reading her thoughts, making her feel uneasy. Bill's dog Max, the Airedale, spread out across the floor. They were comfortable friends.

The forecast was awful. Drifting snow was expected. They had made the trip to Stafford many times; however, the fear of being stranded on the motorway in freezing conditions, made her phone and cancel. She was sorry and annoyed at having to change her plans. She was quiet.

She didn't waste her day and started by making a batch of chocolate muffins, then went off for a swim. At the counter she purchased a new swimming hat, replacing the one that she had carelessly ripped the previous Sunday. The lady apologized, saying that she only had orange hats left. She laughed, saying that she would look like a floating marker buoy, bobbing about having escaped its moorings. It would have to do until she bought another. Once home, a full English breakfast set them up for the day, followed by the muffins, still warm with oozy chocolate. She walked with her son. He said that he felt clean after his shower, using a clean flannel and towel, stepping out onto a clean bathmat instead of the dark mottled vinyl he had been used to, knowing that it wasn't really clean and many tenants had stood on it. She was surprised to hear him say that he liked her gentle, raindrop shower, as he had always preferred a power shower blast. She tried wearing her stripy hat to tame her hair but it was snatched off her head and blown away. Her son ran after it and retrieved it from a grassy bank where it had finally stopped rolling along and got caught on a twig. They walked at a furious pace, buffeted and at times struggling against the wind. Their trousers stuck themselves to their legs. The waves whipped up and crashed onto the concrete wall of the balancing lakes. Her son did not like the waves thrown against the wall and didn't like that part of the walk. Across the path, wavy lines of debris showed where the recent flooding had receded and left its mark. She told her son that the clusters of flowers near the water's edge were primroses. To her, it didn't seem right that they were there. They were not wild but had been planted and did not give the same joy as truly wild primroses snuggling in the hedgerow. The children who walked past them, who had never seen them really wild, might assume that that was how they grew, yet had they not been planted they might not have delighted in them at all. Would they notice them? Celandines were everywhere, clinging where they could, opening their yellow faces to the sun. She reminded her son that his grandmother used to press celandines for handmade birthday cards. For two hours they walked and chatted, dipping into this and that, the bank crisis, dressing tables and learning Russian. Facing into the wind their voices were lost. It was good to see him. Her husband had been out in the garden all day, making good use of the time that hadn't been planned.

Brian, who lived opposite, had a key to her neighbour's house. Her neighbour was away visiting her daughter near Yeovil and had been collected on Thursday evening by her son-in-law. Earlier in the day she had heard an unfamiliar bleep, in fact three bleeps in a row. She listened. There they were again. Her husband had heard them too and went around the house trying to identify and eliminate sounds. He checked anything with a battery. He even got a glass from the kitchen cupboard and pressed it to the wall, like a real detective. The bleeps were definitely coming from next door. Brian unlocked both doors. It didn't feel quite right walking into Evelyn's house. Everything was a mirror image of her own, the television in the corner by the window, the settee in the same position. She didn't like to look at anything. There was nothing out of place in the room. It was immaculate. She greatly admired Evelyn's domestic order. She knew that her own domesticity was often lacking. She stood with Brian in the sitting room, waiting for the bleeps. Sure enough, three bleeps, definitely along the party wall. They listened again. The bleeps came from the top of the cabinet. Brian fetched a chair from the dining room; he held it while she climbed up. It was the control box for the central heating system. Brian took it away to remove the failing batteries. She returned the chair to the dining room. Brian locked the door.

The rugby was on the television. In the top left-hand corner she read that 'Lee' and 'New' were playing. Even the players were finding the wind carried the ball unexpectedly, changing the shape of the game. She would never get used to the flat wide screen in front of her. She saw footballers and newsreaders and chefs and gardeners as intruders, uninvited guests in her front room. Their real-life size was intimidating and made her feel uneasy. The wall to wall, in your face, 24/7 television commercialism was not her. The television was out of keeping with the room; it did not suit the chintzy chairs and the Laura Ashley wallpaper. She was so distressed that for at least a week she refused to go in the front room, except to open the curtains into the morning. It had been a welcome-home present when they returned from Kefalonia last summer. She was sure that her husband had been part of the plan and had enlisted their son to install it while they were away. She never did get to the bottom of it. Both her husband and son denied all knowledge of a conspiracy. There was a small television in the other room, which she watched, if desperate, but her eyes were not what they were and it seemed unsociable not being with her husband. Whatever was on, she put up with it.

Blizzard conditions with a biting wind and driving snow spoilt the day. It had been expected, and although the snow didn't settle, it was raw and cold. She popped out in the car to Bargain Booze. The wind roared in the trees as she parked in the new car park, completed only the other day. How long would it stay so neat, the landscaping newly planted, the wooden barrier in front of the parking bays unbroken? After deciding on three bottles of wine, the man behind the counter suggested that she reconsidered, encouraging her to go for the special offer. Indeed it was a bargain at Bargain Booze. Once home, she stayed in the kitchen, the warmest room. The lights went on and off all day as snow clouds darkened then rushed away to the left leaving a temporary patch of blue and her kitchen bleached with light. In between whisking up a syllabub and preparing vegetables, she sat warming herself in the sunbeams as they came and went, looking out on the wintry scene. Next morning there was an eerie silence. Through the gap in the curtains she could see from her pillow, gentle spiralling flakes. She jumped out of bed and looking out could see that a layer of perfectly white, undisturbed virgin snow had fallen. Later, listening to the occasional car going past, she was glad that she didn't have to drive anywhere in the slippery, slushy conditions. By lunchtime the white world had disappeared. It hadn't been much of a day.

Before going for a swim she made a batch of scones, the ultimate comfort food, truly indulgent with a dollop of double cream. Making them was relaxing – gently rubbing the margarine with the flour until it looked crumby and fell through her fingers like sand. It was therapeutic. It was snowing again and she decided against taking the car, her husband's car, to the pool. Instead, she would walk and take the new path, the 'circular' route. It had always been a path, but it was narrow and muddy and inclined dangerously towards the river. Years ago, she used it as a short cut and remembers her bike slithering on the greasy mud, slipping from beneath her. Her precious son had tipped out of his seat behind her, into a bed of stinging nettles. She gathered him up and kissed him and said sorry so many times she lost count. Nanny hadn't liked the path; it led into a copse, the copse that her friend Chris was campaigning to save from the developers when the new pool was built. Nanny preferred taking the long way round when she took her grandchildren to the pool because there might be hooligans lurking in the trees. The pine trees looked tired. Ivy had latched on and consumed the trunks, a couple had fallen, leaning precariously. Underfoot was rough, made up of brambles and briars. She had supported her friend's efforts to save the trees but really when she looked at them, were they worth saving?

The brief Easter break had thrown her completely. All week she had felt indifferent and withdrawn. Each day got progressively worse. There was nothing worth seeing at the cinema and she felt cheated, dished out of her weekly habit. It had become a habit. She and her friends looked forward to choosing a film, meeting in the car park at four and being blissfully entertained for an hour and a half. Thursday was particularly bad. She had to cover a drama teacher's absence. When she saw the group she didn't fancy her chances. It was the animals, and although they couldn't read and write, they read her thoughts and had her written off before she read out the brief. They had to get into groups of five and each member had to be a character. They had to show their sketch to the class at the end. Simple enough really. Well, they hid in the curtains and turned out the lights and screamed at the tops of their voices. They were uncontrollable, totally off the wall. Nothing she said improved the mayhem. She was relieved that the drama room was like a black padded cell. As if the animals needed to do drama. Thankfully, Friday loomed, but it didn't pass without Livi being sent to the top of the grey stairs. The final straw was when she went to pull her hair. How she had lasted that long she didn't know. She had talked through the entire exam. Her behaviour had been dire. She had hoped that she would burn herself out or simply give up and get on quietly. Suddenly, with half an hour to go, she wanted to go to the toilet, and she went on and on, ranting and raving. She didn't give in. She did not allow her to go to the toilet. She felt that attention-seeking Livi must have an ulterior motive to cause as much trouble as possible. Livi's disruptive behaviour had spoilt her day, which, until then, had been good. In the morning she had taken her exam group to Starbucks to experience café life. It had been different and she hoped the visit would be remembered on the 22nd May when they sat tense and nervous in the restricting exam conditions of the sports hall, trying to remember.

She more than made up for her poor week on Saturday and triumphantly crossed off her "to-do" list, sixty-five year eight exam papers, one hour before breakfast, two hours after, a swim, then lunch, then a straight six hours. It was gruelling. But it was done. Crazy spellings brought a smile, "civ" and "siv" and "shiver" for "sieve"; "soor" and "soring" for "saw" and "sawing"; and they made "strate" or "strayt" lines "wiv" a "'rula".

About nine o'clock her husband went round the house moving all the clocks on an hour. It was as though he had reached a goal, claiming that it would be light until eight o'clock on Sunday evening. He could not contain his excitement. That was it until October. They went to bed at ten o'clock. It was really nine o'clock. So when she got up at six, it was really five. Why had there not been time to see her friend? She had said she would call and see her back in January when they had met in the queue in the building society. Why had it taken so long? Thankfully, when she saw her on Sunday morning, her greyness had gone. There was brightness in her voice and on her face. She was stronger and not depending on the walking sticks. It was time to slough off the skin of winter. There was everything to live for on that sunny morning, the first day of spring.

Despite her optimism, there was a whole week ahead before the holidays. It did not pass without incident.

She tolerated the animals, glad that it was their last lesson with her. On Thursday one came back to find that a piece of cake left in the fridge since Monday had been binned. "It was all dried up," she said.

"All dried up, like you then, Miss." Such bravado. The intense pressure to finalize the coursework caused some friction between her and a colleague. She was confident that her pupils would be finished but he threw a wobbly and had what was termed "an eye-popping moment". It was not pleasant.

A rash of apologies were delivered to her classroom. The animals from the drama lesson peered in and rattled the handle on her locked door demanding attention, distracting her and spoiling the goodbye lunch arranged for a colleague. Quickly she skimmed over them. Their letters meant nothing to her. She knew they didn't care. Not for one moment did she believe what they had written. They were insincere and thick with sarcasm.

Her two daft friends sang happy birthday to her. Immediately she felt terrible. She thought she had forgotten someone's birthday. They insisted that she undid her present so that they could see her face. It was a pair of kitchen scissors. She had said that in all her thirty-five years of marriage she had never had a pair. Well, not entirely true, her husband had bought her a pair, but they were left-handed and she didn't count them. They laughed. They were good friends. Her left-handed son was going to be the beneficiary of the left-handed scissors.

As she knew they would, her pupils finished their work on Friday morning. There had been no need for all that anger earlier in the week. As usual, in the afternoon, Livi was chewing gum and she asked her nicely to put it in the bin. Livi stood by the bin dividing the gum with her teeth. She spat half the gum into the bin. "And the rest," she said, watching her. Reluctantly the rest was dropped from her mouth. Livi must have thought that she was the worst person on earth, like everyone else seemed to think this week. Livi took herself off and sat with her feet up on the long wooden bench by the door, hidden by the blazers, her thumb in her mouth, sulking. Her melancholy haze of the past fortnight began to lift and she found herself looking at the clock. Only an hour to go.

April

The sun was setting. A band of cloud lay between the earth and the clear evening sky. "Sometimes," she said, "the cloud looks like the sea, still and deep, like it does now." She could see the horizon in the distance and imagined boats. "It could be the sea." Wanting her son to see it as she saw it. "Sometimes the clouds look like bare craggy mountains," she continued. "When the cloud is rough and stacked up in the distance. Like looking down on the Alps." In her mind she was always making something out of something else. In real life she did it too, whether it was left-over food or clothing past its best. Her kitchen door curtain, which had shrunk in the wash, had been rendered useful again with a cuff of denim from a pair of her old jeans, which before that had been her son's old jeans. Curtains became tablecloths. In fact, when she used to make her own clothes, they were made with the intention of changing them into another piece of clothing in years to come. She liked the challenge of being thrifty and resourceful, making something out of nothing.

A power nap had revived her and instead of going to bed she arranged her marking in neat piles on the dining room table, ready for the morning. She tapped the sheets and paper clipped them to secure. On Saturday she marked. She could see herself finishing.

The professor had written. "An absolutely outstanding student." That called for a celebratory couple of bottles of wine. No longer articulate, she didn't finish the marking. She woke to find the world white. Pink petals and snow whirled and fell silently. Excitedly, her absolutely outstanding son made a snowman, revealing strips of bright green grass as he rolled the ball around the garden. He lifted him onto the garden seat and gave him some twigs for arms. She called him Mr Snow, if there ever was a Mr Snow in the Mr Men series. The marking, started on Thursday night, was finally finished on Sunday afternoon. The holiday ahead was all hers.

Earlier that morning she had made a start on "spring cleaning". The curtains had gone to the cleaners, she had been to the bank and she had been for a swim. It was as she reversed her car on the drive that her son opened the door, waving an A4 envelope. Receiving anything other than junk mail and circulars on a Monday was unusual. Getting the letter changed the shape of the day. The plan to blitz the house fell by the wayside. She jumped about the kitchen, shrieking and sighing while her son made coffee to celebrate. They hugged and hugged again. He was so pleased for her. Saying that she was pleased with herself was an understatement. With all the laughing, the dry chlorine glaze across her face broke into a million hairline cracks and she went upstairs to fix it. Returning, she sat down, her hands trembled as she read.

The two of them took themselves off to The Black Horse for a "real" celebration. Once again striding off along the Railway Walk, rank in places where dog owners had been too lazy to remove the shit excreted by their pets. The January brownness had recovered. Vigorous fresh green shoots reached towards the light. In a month's time the path would be fringed with dancing cow parsley, a veil of white flowers gently swaying in the breeze, the hawthorn blossom stifling. They chatted mainly about the letter, the conversation becoming at times out of control. It would be a summer read, the book to catch the eye at the airport bookshop. On offer, buy two get one free, a bold yellow sticker on the cover. Even Steve Wright was mentioned and, worse still, Richard and Judy. The market was competitive; publishers would go to great lengths to promote a new title and shift stock. She was modest and could not envisage anything so ridiculous. The glass of white wine hit the spot. Walking home, her shoulder bag slipped from her shoulder. Narrow sloping shoulders prevented her wearing it over one shoulder and so she wore the bag across her body, leaving her arms free to carry shopping, which was rare, hold a rail, or simply push her hands in her pockets. Weeks ago she noticed the strap pulling from the seam and knew then it deserved a stitch. Idly messing about with the strap, she decided to cut it. It changed the style completely, obviously now a handbag, and took it to Smarts to be fixed. The bell rang as she pushed open the door. The L-shaped counter was completely covered in a muddle of shoes and boots. A sweaty pungent leathery smell greeted her, along with the whining sound of a machine, a cross between a bacon slicer and a sander, which trimmed and smoothed the heels and soles. She handed the cobbler her bag, explaining what she needed and he handed her a pink ticket. She was not good with handbags. It was another thing to think about and look after, whereas a shoulder bag was worn, an extension of a coat or jacket, less obvious. A handbag was less casual and revealed far more about her.

The euphoria gradually subsided. All through the winter she had waited for a letter. Catching a glimpse of the postman's reflective jacket in her road was enough to set her heart racing. On a school day it was her burning desire to check the post as she opened the front door, scanning the doormat for an interesting postmark, forever hopeful. Her philosophy was that no news was good news and now that she had her good news she felt strangely empty. There was no pleasing her. Her first manuscript had been drafted on A4 paper folded into quarters, each section tightly packed with words. For her second manuscript she had invested in a notebook, A6 size, small enough to fit into a bag or pocket, ready to note. Its drawback was when she came to type what she had written. The notebook did not stay open and she had to wedge the dictionary across the spine. The good thing was that notes were orderly and all together, unlike the pieces of paper, which she kept together with a red rubber bands retrieved from the drive, dropped carelessly by the postman. The current use for her collection of rubber bands was tying down the spent daffodils.

Her energy for "spring cleaning" resumed. One of the holiday jobs was to clear the loft of some of the boxes that had accumulated over the past thirty-five years. Clothing, school books, yards of fabric, toys belonging to the children, all stored in the first place in case they were wanted at a later date. At the time she thought that she might reminisce in her later years, that she might spend time poring over her essays and her algebra. Certainly, they brought back memories when she saw them again, but as for keeping them any longer? No, it was time for them to go. Systematically she went through everything her rangy son dropped through the gaping hole in the ceiling. She directed him to where things were from the foot of the ladder. Everything was filthy, covered with a layer of gritty blackness. Years of wind and billowing smoke had got under the tiles from the days when they had a "real" fire. Over the years moths and mice had feasted quietly on her clothes, and they were riddled with holes. A few selected things were kept, mainly because she could not bear to part with the fabrics or the expert craftsmanship, which she knew she would never be able to achieve again. She found the sleeves of a lovely dress that she had unpicked years ago with the intention of changing it to a skirt, but had never done so. She found a bag full of nightdresses. She left them in a pile for her husband to remember. Only the other day they were talking about nightdresses. She had insisted that she used to wear them a long time ago. He wanted her to wear them again. She didn't think she could, preferring the soft freedom of her comfortable pyjamas. She found some old dresses that she had bought second-hand, and hoped that washing them would eliminate the pungent odour that seemed ingrained in everything. A bag of teddies was found, some of which were spared. They had their picture taken on the bathroom floor along with all the other teddies. Her son named them all as they were lined up for the photo shoot. She couldn't throw Froggie away. He had been posted to Longrigg in the Lake

District where her son was on a school trip. No sooner had the bus left than Froggie was remembered. She parcelled him up and sent him first class. The process had diverted her attention from the fact that it was the first time that any of the children had gone away. Then there was Egg, perfectly knitted, his face long gone, half blue and half white, sent from her cousin when her son was born. She couldn't throw Egg away. Then there were two teddies, proper teddies given to the children by their grandma. Apart from those four, all the others were resigned to the black sack. She came across her old hairdryer in its case, the sort that allowed her to walk around within the limits of the flex. It had a flowery hood that fitted over her jumbo rollers and puffed up with warm air to dry her hair. She kept her one and only Valentine card, a few letters and her school Speech Day programmes. They all fitted into an envelope.

Her husband's pile was much bigger: yellowing newspapers, cricket and football snippets from newspapers spilling out of scrapbooks, and quite a few maths books, their orange covers defaced in graffiti and doodles.

When she showed her husband the picture she had found of his football team he became all quiet and emotional. He was in the front row, kneeling, his arms folded across his chest, undoubtedly the youngest, a boy, but a good player, his pace needed on the wing. At the time he had enjoyed the camaraderie and the banter of the older men. She could see him trying to remember their names. By now they would all be retired, having served their purpose in the workplace. All gone. Her husband longed to turn back the clock, to have his time again.

Unlike her husband, she was no longer sentimental about the things she had found. She did not yearn for the things in front of her nor the memories that they gave. Clearing the loft was simply a practical task that needed to be done, before she was unable to do it herself. It was arduous and dirty, and she spent a long time on her hands and knees, locked in position, sifting and sorting. Twice she filled the car and went to the refuse tip to offload the knotted sacks. When she went back the second time, there on the floor beside an upright vacuum cleaner was her hairdrier. How could it have been detected in a knotted sack? The evening

67

brought further memories flooding back. Her husband's head nodded in time with the music playing in the background. "Let's Go to San Francisco" by The Flower Pot Men, "Aquarius" and "Let the Sunshine in", from the musical *Hair* once again got to him. The actors had filtered through the audience, who were waiting in anticipation for the performance to start, he recalled to his son, and Marsha Hunt said to him, "Don't look so sad, honey." She could just make out "Suzanne" by Leonard Cohen; it was one of her favourite sounds and featured on the compilation CD that her son had put together for her birthday a few years ago. It reminded her of being in the sixth form and being collected from school by her husband in his dark green Mini with a white roof. In a way, she did cling to the past, as she was always contrasting then with now. Her husband could not remember the dirge from those days, but he could remember picking her up from school in his car.

She thought that she would cook liver and onions for dinner and once she had posted the cards to her two friends who shared the same birthday as her she went into the very busy, reputable butcher's. She loved the butcher's. It was old-fashioned, raw and basic: bloody wooden boards and wickedly sharp knives. It was where she met people she knew, where people stood long enough to chat. The space for customers was so narrow that even if you didn't know anyone when you went in, you did by the time you left. It was the only shop in the High Street to offer such opportunity. Beef and pork and lamb and chicken and bacon and duck were neatly separated into fields by hedges of plastic parsley. She liked the fact that you could have exactly what you wanted and you got what was there. Not that she did, but she could spend serious money in the butcher's. The butchers on the other side of the counter busied themselves, selecting and cutting, dancing round each other in the confined space. She knew their faces but was served by a man who was unfamiliar. "Half a pound of pig's liver, please." Not displayed. More expensive cuts for the weekend customers: piles of duck breast, the thick white fat neatly wrapped, food for friends, ribs of beef for Sunday lunch, food for families. While the "good for you" liver was being sliced out the back, she looked around. Snuggled behind the smoked bacon were the olives. The green olives were especially good; she would indulge in a pot. There was Diane at the end of the counter. She hadn't seen her since the karting event. "How are you?" she said. She came straight out with it. "My daughter died on Thursday, an asthma attack." Not in a million years had she expected the reply. What could she say? In the narrow space she hugged Diane close, oblivious to people going back and forth through the chain-linked curtain hanging at the door. Tears filled her eyes and rolled down her cheeks. Diane's face stayed the same, staring blankly ahead, looking at nothing. Full of sorrow, they parted.

"That's £1.36, madam."

"And I'll have a pot of green olives please."

Totalling it up on a notepad, he said, "That will be £3.40."

She paid and walked home, crossing the road to walk in the sunny gaps between the houses.

Too much drink on Friday night had rendered her son fragile. He lay in the sitting room, his head on a freshly ironed cushion. He was waiting for a lift to the station. Suddenly, the house was filled with young people, their cars parked haphazardly. They came and everyone left, including her son. It was quiet. She got on with her day. Her thoughts were with Diane. As expected, the olives were good. They didn't reach the fridge, but were eaten straight out of the pot with her fingers each time she passed the kitchen table until they were gone, which didn't take long.

She felt the need to do some baking. She made what she called the "very good orange cake" and an economical barm brack, a robust tea bread made out of left-over tea and in this case left-over dried fruit from Christmas. Soaking in cold tea the night before had restored the tired and dehydrated fruit to its former plump juiciness. Coming in from outside, the kitchen was warm and filled with friendly smells. She tasted both. She could hear the shearing pressure of the ground almonds as her teeth closed over the very good orange cake, a squeaking, moist sensation. Sliced thinly and spread with butter, the barm brack was wholesome and satisfying. As part of her repertoire, she also made a deep chocolate cheesecake. It had no smell. But the taste when she cut into the creamy velvety texture later was dreamy.

Overhead, the skylarks sang, every now and then dropping into the soft springy grass, the harbingers of spring. It didn't feel like spring and she was glad of her stripy hat. Having exhausted the spring-cleaning, she was at a loose end and on the spur of the moment went off with her son to Ivanhoe Beacon. It was part of the Chilterns, a shoulder of land that protruded away from hills, the highest point for miles around. Apart from the parking arrangements, the wildness hadn't changed, the chalky scars where people had walked remained the same. She liked being high, surveying the land, and pointed out to her son the churches of Edlesborough and Totternhoe and Leighton Buzzard. In the far distance were Bow Brickhill woods and beyond, the sprawl of Milton Keynes. In the near distance was the white lion etched into the hillside and at the foot of the Downs were the gliders. It was once a Sunday afternoon pleasure to take a picnic and watch the gliders from the top of the Downs. A small bi-plane would lift the glider into the sky and when high enough people would gasp as the engine noise changed and the rope was released, leaving the glider to float gently back to earth. She remembered the graceful wingspan catching the sunlight, glinting against the blue and counting how many were in the sky at once. They whined as they spiralled in the thermals, catching the warm air currents, lifting them higher and higher.

From there they went to Ashridge and walked amongst the bluebells, admittedly not quite a carpet but, none the less, tips of blue stabbing through the loose dark soil. Peaty tracks took them in all directions. In places, gouged ruts had filled with rainwater. The sweet air was invigorating, like a therapeutic tonic. Inhaling deeply, she filled her lungs, breathing out slowly. Trees had fallen, majestic trees, caught off guard in a rip of wind brought snapping and crashing to the ground, their shallow roots bare and exposed. Apart from the woodpeckers laughing, the woods were silent. She peered into the trees and beyond, hoping to see a deer. She had been privileged to see one once before. Until she saw his big brown eyes looking at her she had been unaware of his presence. He blended in, becoming part of the forest. She felt like an intruder, an uninvited guest, trespassing over his territory. It was a humbling experience and she moved quietly away. They drove along the road at the bottom of the zoo and turned into

Harling Road. It hadn't always been but now it was a rat run, a short cut from over there, missing out a congested corner. Lorries and vans, far too big, drove far too fast along the narrow, winding country road. She slowed and indicated right. Doo Little Lane was a single-track road leading to the Mill. She and her husband used to walk as lovers along the lane, holding hands, stopping to kiss. The Mill snuggled in the safety of the Ouzel, a mere stream that eventually flowed within twenty yards of where she lived now. The pool at the back of the Mill was still and deep, the yard at the front was rough and unkempt, tufts of grass and weeds grew between the cobbles. She remembered playing at the spring where the Ouzel sprung out of the ground below the Downs. She and her sister removed their socks and sandals and paddled around, their feet turning blue in the icy cold water. She stopped at the church, seen from the Beacon earlier, and pulled into the car park. Apart from the birds, they had the churchyard to themselves, familiar and comfortable.

"That is where your Grandma is, if you ever need to know," she said, remembering that Saturday morning in January. The turf had still not knitted together. "Let's walk round the churchyard." It was earthy and wet. Primroses were everywhere, pockets of gentle yellow. She looked for her Godmother's grave. She would have had a headstone. It was as she remembered on that hot September day, wearing her black linen dress. She was always known as Dorothy, but her name was actually Elsie Dorothy. She had forgotten. Next to her was a name she remembered, though not fondly, not surprisingly a spinster, a friend of her mother's. She had seen all she needed.

She sat in her dressing gown at the kitchen table. The smell of kippers drifted over the entire house. A pile of mainly square-shaped cards had accumulated in the past few days and she sat undoing them, guessing the handwriting on the envelope. They were good cards and she set them up on the mantelpiece in the dining room. Besides the cards there were two presents: a pair of earrings from her sister and an amazing necklace from her son, the son sitting at the table, enjoying the kippers with her. Her husband didn't enjoy kippers; he wasn't partial to fiddling with the bones. His breakfast was getting cold. Eventually, when he did appear, he was nonchalant, as though it was any day of the week. He didn't even say happy birthday to her and give her a squeeze. He had warned her the previous day that he hadn't bought a present and he hadn't got a card. The stone ornament that had been earmarked hers had been sold. It had been on display for two years and he sold it to a woman on the very day that he was going to buy it for her. He tried to cover his shame by lightly saying that he thought he had done quite well sorting out the anniversary present and the Christmas present. He could tell that she was not impressed. She was disappointed, not only for herself but for him too and wondered why, when it always made him feel so good when he bought her something nice, he hadn't bothered.

During the day she had been to the bin at the side of the house and from there she could see something on the grass and went to check. It was a duck. It was not unusual for ducks to come into the garden on her birthday. It was asleep in the shelter of the hedge. Even later, when she mentioned it to her husband, the duck was still there, but stood up and lamely waddled under the hedge. While they were having dinner he went to see if the duck was there and reported that it had gone. Wondering if her husband was just saying that to pacify, she and her son went out to see for themselves. The beam of her son's head torch was thrown across the garden and behind the hedge. True enough, the duck had recovered and gone. In the darkness she gathered her swimsuit and towel from the line. She would need them in a few hours' time. Having cleared the dining room of debris, she sat once again at the table in the kitchen, sharing the dregs of the Christmas port in the miniature glasses bought from a tabletop sale years ago. Truly there was nothing left to drink except cold beer. Neither of them needed anything else to drink. Both were completely drunk, past knowing or caring that it was time to stop. They just didn't want the evening to end. The fluorescent numbers on the oven clock blinked 1.14 a.m.

The holiday was rapidly coming to an end. Monday was looming. Last week it had seemed a long way off, now it was imminent. Despite the cold easterly wind, she set to in the garden. The robin was never far from her elbow. She talked to the robin and he listened, his head cocked attentively. He fluttered around, looking for grubs in the freshly turned soil.

She made her way down to Canary Wharf. She went in case the publishers summoned her to a meeting at short notice and she needed to know where to go. The decision of what to wear had bothered her. Years ago she possessed an old stone-coloured cotton coat. Although it soaked up the rain and was anything but warm, it had a worn, beaten look that she liked. A ripped pocket had rendered it useless without major repair and so it had been cast into a black sack to be recycled. The day before she had had the house to herself and messed about in front of the mirror trying all her trousers with a particular jacket. Not happy with any, she resorted to the faithful old jeans that were well past their best, getting paler by the wash and more and more threadbare. On the morning, she unbolted the back door and tested the temperature. She wanted to get it right. It was freezing and in the end decided to wear her coat, but kept the clothes beneath to a minimum. Standing, waiting to be served, she was exasperated by dithering indecision, least of all in her. She used to say to her children, when there was a choice, "Yes or no." Right until the last moment when the voice on the Tannoy called her to window 2 she was undecided about which ticket to buy. In her head she worked out all the different combinations of possibilities. She knew the price of the ticket. Just get it. She nearly always chose the more expensive ticket, because it offered more choice and she could afford it, even though she didn't always use the service. All she wanted was the first train to get her there.

Even though it was running late, she paid for and caught a Virgin train, wanting to be in the thick of it by nine. Having stood for the entire journey before, she collapsed into the first available seat. She was on the wrong side of the carriage. She wanted to see Ivanhoe Beacon and the copper ball of the Bridgewater monument through the canopy. Turning her head she tried looking, but the girl opposite was watching her. Soon it was too late and she settled to look out over the fields, then in a split second of darkness the tunnel through the Chilterns, then Watford, then the sidings at Willesden Junction, then minding the gap at Euston station.

She had never been to Canary Wharf, but had seen it in the distance from the top of St Paul's Cathedral and the top of the London Eye and of course on television. The cluster of buildings contrasted severely with the immediate surroundings. No expense had been spared. Granite steps, sculptures and water features designed and built for smart clean living for those in sharp suits, whose job it was the keep the city on its toes, the business centre of the universe. Glass, concrete and steel penetrated the murky sky, exposed to the cold east wind blowing in along the Thames. Even on a hot day, it would be cool, long ribs of shadow stretching out across the landscaped areas, office workers glad to return to the temperature-controlled, tinted-glass offices to thaw out and warm up.

Taking the Central Line, she went west. It had been four weeks since she had been window-shopping in Kensington High Street. In all that time the clothes she had seen had remained in her mind. The layout in the shop had changed. The blue checked dress that had drawn her deeper into the shop was no longer displayed and there was no sign of the cocoa-coloured crinkled skirt. She selected a different skirt and a soft pink cardigan to match. Holding them over her arm, she continued to search through the rails for the clothes in her mind. An assistant could see that she was purposeful and asked if she needed help. She explained that the skirt had gone and so had the dress. The assisstant calmed and reassured her, and disappeared into the stockroom. To see the assistant returning with the items brought a smile to her face. She was unsure about the dress; she didn't want to look like mutton, or lamb, just herself. She tried on everything. All, except the dress, was neatly folded and wrapped in yellow tissue at the counter and placed in a big glossy carrier bag. Never was a bag more revealing than when she returned to the east to meet up with her son. She felt embarrassed, ashamed of her extravagance, when the people around her hadn't enough to pay the rent. It was obvious to her that compared to the local people she was affluent, with money to spend on frivolities such as clothes. She herself felt inconspicuous in the High Street but how she wanted a Lidl bag instead of the bright yellow poppies at the end of her arm. As though she had crossed a border, she was thankful to be back in the west.

They took a table by the window looking out onto Earlham Street. The steely grey sky had not let up all day. Above her, the buildings and cranes reached into the fusion pressing down, spoiling Saturday. Not once did the sun break through and raise a smile on the buttoned-up grimness. The three of them exchanged their news and her sons checked recent pictures on their cameras while they waited to be fed. The food was good and filled her starving children. Not for a moment did they think that the desserts were made on the premises as they claimed, not even cut up on the premises, just served directly from a cardboard box. She decided not to go with them to the music shop across the road and said her goodbyes outside the restaurant. For the record, they each took pictures and they kissed goodbye. Eventually, when the sky could hold out no longer, thick drizzle brought the umbrellas out, jostling for position over the shiny pavements. She walked back to the station, not minding the dampness in her hair.

Now that she had some new clothes she felt inclined to be ruthless and reduce the pile of loft-infested clothes to a minimum. Would she really wear them? She thought that the nightdresses could go. On her husband's suggestion one night she had tried the yellow one. She did not like lying in its twisted folds, nor did she like seeing her aging silhouette against the light, nor of the feel on waking, of her thighs sticking together. Thankfully, she did not experience the worst feeling of all, her nightdress being lifted. They could go. It was depressing and demoralizing seeing the clothes heaped on the floor, that once had fitted so well, needing drastic alteration to enable them to be worn again, and she proceeded to reduce the pile still further. The shroud of grey continued.

Most days she thought about her mother. It had been two years since she died on that bright sunny April morning, a morning just like the one when she had been born, just like the one today. She wasn't sad or gloomy. In fact, when she drove round a particular roundabout on the way to school it brought a

75

positive smile to her face as it did most days, as though there was a wicked sense of humour about the dying experience. She remembered the wreath of spring flowers snuggled carefully, like the spare wheel under the back seat, the ideal spot. The momentum of driving round the roundabout brought the seat crashing down. She pulled up sharp in a bus stop lay-by, got out of the car and lifted the seat. In disbelief she saw the crushed stalks, concertinaed, macramé-style and flattened flowers. Surely the three-second rule applied. Carefully she prised them upright again and tightly tied the seat to the headrest with her swipe card lanyard. What more could she do? She realized that it wasn't until she had got older that she had given her mother much thought. Looking back, she seemed to think that her mother would stay the same, like she was when she had got married and left home: independent, fit and able. She didn't seem to notice when it was that she was no longer like that. She pictured her going about her day, making soup or going to the shops on the bus. When did she stop doing those things?

On Tuesday after lunch she checked her pigeonhole. There was a message, hand written on recycled paper. Something had arrived in the post. The message was from her son and it had been taken at 10.53 a.m. She had to phone. Over the phone he read out the letter. She did not want heads to turn, listening to her conversation and tried not to seem excited. It was the contract from the publishers. The shroud of grey had lifted and the sun came out. As light as air she sprang from pupil to pupil, generously repeating what needed to be done. Once home she read the documents for herself and signed on the dotted line.

She expected a taunting picket line of activists stoking a fire of old school desks in a rusty oil drum, booing and throwing eggs, calling her a scab and lots of other things besides. Banners and placards raised high, fighting for the cause. It was none of those outside her school. In fact it was eerily quiet. Usefully she used her day to shred and recycle the volumes of paper associated with education.

They left their house of thirty-five years and moved to Chingford in North-east London. They gave up all they had for a furnished flat in a tower block. When she pulled back the curtains she could see across London. She could see the famous landmarks.

Instead of dreaming, she should have got up at six o'clock, when she looked at the time, and got on with her marking.

On the pale pink walls of the bedroom were two doilies with a flash of pink ribbon from bridesmaid's dresses. She and her husband went for a walk and stood as newcomers to the neighbourhood, talking to the local people. Grassy mounds and paths divided the blocks of flats. Where was the garden? Where would she set up her deck chair and turn her face to the sun? Where would her husband reap and plough and scatter seeds?

She could tell the ones that had gone off the boil. They walked into her room with nothing more than a handbag containing the essentials, the mobile phone and the hairbrush, or, in the case of the boys, a man bag or more usually no bag at all, nothing that couldn't contain an A4 exercise book or a textbook. They had heard the word text because they were continually checking them. She heard lame excuses. "I thought it was Tuesday." "I left it at my Dad's." Pathetic. Different tacks were tried towards the end of the course to keep the pupils alert to the immediacy of the exams. It was the time of year when her exam group was leaving. Leaving to make their way in the world. Many of the pupils she had known for four years. She had watched them grow up from quiet, timid children to assertive, confident young people. Admittedly, that really applied to the girls, the boys were the same, just much taller. It was the last day that they would be together as a group and she became quite nostalgic. She reminded them that in August that feeling of success would tear through them. They would screech and cry and throw their arms around each other when they got their results. Friends and family would send them cards congratulating them. She read out some cards, used as props for such an occasion, followed by tongue-in-cheek anecdotes on the naff selection of cards.

Her eight-mile journey to school was changing. Slowly, ever so slowly, so slowly it could hardly be noticed, the trees along the wide grassy ways and streets were gradually unfolding before her eyes. Transforming from their stark winter silhouettes to a soft downy green, leaves fluttering and dancing, blurring the edges and obscuring the hard landscape behind, greedily growing, reaching upwards and outwards filling up the promising pink morning.

"Happy go lucky" had finally reached the big screen. They had seen the trailer weeks ago. She wondered if it had enough about it, similar in many ways to the ups and downs of her own life, mirroring the good fortune or the bad luck. There didn't seem to be a storyline, just a lot of individual happenings in a day, probably exaggerated for better viewing.

May

Election fever was in the air. She had plenty of thoughts about the subject, but didn't go to vote. It had been three years since she had taken her mother to vote. She had insisted and she had wheeled her in the wheelchair on a glorious May afternoon to the local school used as a polling station. A staunch Labourite for her entire life, her mother took her by surprise and voted Conservative.

The heat of the fire and too much red wine rendered her pleasantly useless. She fought against the comatose state, determined to enjoy every moment with her friends, but by early Saturday morning she had to give in. Feeling fragile after only five hours sleep she sat fixing her face in the spare room. Ramsey the cat sat on the windowsill. He was taking a keen interest in the animals in the garden on the other side of the lane. Bored after a while and wanting attention, he left his spot on the sill, reaching her lap via the desk. His claws splayed as he circled, digging into her thighs through her jeans until he curled up. Settled, he shut his eyes. He was not asleep. Finishing her face, she shook him off. The most amazing breakfast anchored her stomach. Like teenagers they went out for the day in a sporty Saab, the roof down and The Rolling Stones blaring. Any cobwebs from the night before blown away. Her hair, pressed down with a colourful cloche, escaped and whipped about, stinging her face like grits of sand. They stopped off here and there like regular "old" people. They went to Bakewell and bought a pudding. They went to the farm shop at Chatsworth and bought some local sausages. They went to Oakes's reclaim yard to buy a stone lady for the garden. There was none. They went to Patchwork Direct, an Aladdin's Cave of fabrics and haberdashery. Moving from shelf to shelf, her eyes wide, she scanned. It was good to talk to the man behind the counter, to someone with technical knowledge and a love for fabrics. She went around like a child alone in a sweet shop. Resisting was hard and even though she knew that it would lie folded in a drawer forever, she bought a length of checked cotton. Back in the car, they went to Ilam, where a few years ago her son and his contemporaries had exhibited their raw art using few materials other than those gleaned from the wild, left in situ at the end for the elements to decompose and change.

They talked way into the night. Husbands, heavy with sleep and alcohol, had said goodnight hours ago. "Tell me about your writing," said her friend. She had started to write in her head years ago but it had taken great courage actually to start writing with a pen. It wasn't her, and at times she felt silly. Never without folded A4 paper and pen she wrote in her smallest handwriting waiting for the potatoes to boil or on the train – anywhere, in fact. Somehow she felt secretive, as though she shouldn't be putting what was in her mind down on paper. She felt disloyal to those she was writing about. It was uncomfortable. When she said that she was writing a book, people were sceptical. It was a whim and she knew they didn't believe her. She knew what they were thinking. It would come to nothing. They would laugh years later "Where's that book you were writing?" Her story was every bit as good as some she had read. It was better than some she had read. She had a story to tell and writing it down was her medium, expressing her thoughts freely without ridicule, without interruption, with no one judging her, or tell her it was wrong or stupid. Having lived a lie for so long, whatever she wrote had to be sincere and honest. She was strangely attracted to writing about the incidental mundane things that made up life, which usually went unnoticed. Her quiet nature gave the impression that she had nothing much to say, when quite the opposite was true. Over the years she had come to the opinion that people didn't really know each other at all, even people quite close didn't "really" know each other. Apart from getting her thoughts down, it was a good way of learning and using new words, words that she had never written before. It was a good way of improving her spellings, always a failing of hers and it was a good way of staying alert and keeping her memory sharp.

She was suspicious of people who walked on grass verges. Trespassing. Somehow they looked furtive, looking behind them as they stumbled and hurried along, their feet wet, their trousers darkening, absorbing the dampness from the grass as though migrating or displaced, transient and usually carrying a bag that bumped the side of their leg. They had probably missed the bus and were hoping for another, turning to see if there was one. But that made them look anxious and even dishonest, vulnerable, like some desperado or a vagrant or car delivery man who had delivered his car and was walking in order to economize with his personalized red and white number plate under his arm.

When she said to her son, "What shall I cook for your birthday?" he said, "Well, what about a Chinese?"

On and off she spent the entire day in the kitchen. It was the hottest day, not one to be slaving over a hot stove. A whole range of books lay open on the kitchen table. Unfamiliar recipes were exacting and she needed to keep reading them, checking quantities and the method. There was a lot of preparation, making marinades and batters and slicing vegetables and stirring sauces and shelling prawns. Gradually as the sun fell over the kitchen, the blind was pulled down lower and lower, keeping out the dazzling light. Towards the end – and she went way over time – the oven was on, the grill was on and all the gas rings were on. Like Friday nights in the local take-away there was fierce last-minute stir-frying and frantic coming together of ingredients. She felt that she had just taken a massive order jotted on a "Post it", nos. 23, 31, 58, 131, 136 and 142. But instead of tin foil trays in a carrier bag it was served up in the garden in her generous dishes with freezing cold lagers. Quietly impressed, she sat back, graciously accepting the award-winning comments. From the empty dishes and the fit-to-burst feeling everyone was experiencing she took that to mean that the Chinese meal had been a success and it had all been worth while. Meatballs had been requested for the next birthday dinner, a whole lot easier.

How do they make films like Forgetting Sarah Marshall and get away with it? Definitely not turned on by Peter's sheer nakedness or the farcical cavorting around. Absolute crap.

She decided to risk wearing her high heels with her legs bare. By lunchtime she was suffering, limping around cautiously, every part of her feet causing grimacing pain. Out of sight, she sat with her feet in a washing-up bowl filled with cold water. A thrilling feeling travelled from her feet to her stomach on up to her brain, though she rather doubted that she had one, thinking that it was feasible to wear the shoes in the first place. She sat enjoying the cooling feeling, absently staring at the bookshelf opposite, taking in the random spines staring back at her. Thinking that she caught a glimpse of a library label, she stood up and paddling water across the floor, reached for the book. Sure enough, the missing book. Pleased to have found it, she took it back to the library. Once returned, she crossed the library to the fiction section. There on the top shelf was *Captain Corelli's Mandolin*, and there on the spine, trapped under the protective see-through cover, were grains of sand from Katelios. Removing the book, she smiled to herself, holding the fond memories in her hands.

The weather turned warm and summery. Marking exam papers in the garden was infinitely better than marking indoors. "The shefs added hurbs to the mints beef." It made her cringe. There was no hope.

Her spaghetti bolognaise was on the back burner, simmering. He didn't mean to, but the boy in the adjacent kitchen lifted the lid on his gas cooker too roughly. The force brought her lid crashing down and sent her pan of bolognaise flying off the cooker, spilling the contents down her new beaded skirt before landing on the floor. For once, she was speechless. She wiped it as best as she could with her apron while the class clattered about with the saucepans.

She came home, glad to have finished the latest round of marking. Her husband had taken the day off. He was quiet. He had wasted his time and hadn't settled to anything. He had spent the day aimlessly walking in and out of the house and about the house, going into all the rooms, every now and then shaking his head from side to side and sighing heavily, looking around, moving to the window and looking out onto the road, aware of cars going too fast (in spite of the recent calming measures) or out onto the garden surveying what he had achieved, wondering where all the time had gone, traipsing bits of grass and clippings everywhere. He was melancholy and she could sense his frustration, and although she herself looked forward to a day of solitude away from the usual hubbub, she didn't think it suited her husband to be on his own all day. He needed routine and shape to his day. His tongue was furred and breath stale, his appearance unkempt, not even bothering for when she came home. Understandably, he had nothing much to say and one-sided conversation was hard going. Quietly, she got on with the dinner.

"Well," she said to her friend, "does it smell of the loft?" Judy held the dress and, breathing deeply, she sniffed. She didn't need to say anything, she could see it in her eyes. She suggested another wash, perhaps with fabric conditioner. She said she would try but loathed the smell of conditioners. In fact she was not keen on any synthetic smells like air fresheners used in plugs or toilet blocks that clip to the side of the bowl, odour eaters or smelly trees hanging from the rear-view mirror in cars. But she would have another go. She could see the piles from the loft shrinking further. Maybe she should just bin the lot. The fun had been getting it all out of the boxes and bags in the loft.

Regardless of the weather, she went out in the garden to tackle the weeding, starting with the border along the path that had become overgrown with dandelions and chickweed. Years ago, when the hedge was nothing more than saplings and you could see into next door's garden through the chain link fencing, she used to weed it regularly, but it had grown so vigorously that weeds had been denied the light. Severe pruning and cutting back last summer, however, had allowed them to grow freely again. Then she cut the grass. Getting into position to go up and down with the mower brought comment from her husband. She could have done without it, remembering a similar comment once before, when she walked away, leaving the mower standing in the middle of the uncut grass. She lined up the bags of weeds by the shed ready for the trip to the dump and moved nearer the house to continue the onslaught. Shards of glass still glinted amongst the gravel as she weeded on her hands and knees, tugging at the beastly violets, their rhizome network of roots holding fast. Lost in thought, memories of that Saturday afternoon came into her mind. How her son's hand had survived without a graze was beyond her. She and her husband were waiting for their friends to arrive. They were coming for tea, a proper old-fashioned sit-down tea of egg-and-cress sandwiches neatly cut into triangles with the crusts removed, and meringues filled with cream. She was putting the finishing touches to the table when suddenly a brittle, splintering sound rained down. Why had his pent up anger caused such violence? They tried, but couldn't concentrate on their friends. They were too distracted by the incident. It was as though their eldest son hadn't wanted the friends to come, meaning that he would lose his parents' undivided attention, like a spoilt child unwilling to share. She knew in her heart that it would have been better to sort it out there and then for them and for their son, not leave it festering. But it wasn't their way. Both had come from families where abuse was normal and they had learnt to just get on with it. They didn't question. Like his father, her son was never easy to talk to at the best of times; they were too close and antagonized each other and so the subject was dropped and never spoken about again. She loved her son dearly and had given up everything for him. She did so regret not being able to talk to freely without him getting defensive and angry. She was disappointed with herself, remembering how it felt, having no one to talk to. She thought that he paid no attention when she took her husband a cup of tea before she left for work, putting it down on the round grass mat beside the bed. He just grunted as she said

"Goodbye, see you later," and laid her hand on his folded arm or his thigh heaving under the covers. But he would open his eyes as she turned to go, seeing her fresh and clean, ready for her day, her hair brushed and falling around. She thought wrong.

It was time for the curry lesson again and she needed some more vegetables. She selected a range of pods and roots, fruits and flowers and for school she needed ten bottles of "wul", washing up liquid for those who don't know the language of supermarkets. She bagged it ready in a "bag for life". As she moved to the checkout she could feel her hackles rise. Joan was on the only till open. She had come across Joan before and since then had avoided her. She wasn't good at customer care and expected you to put the items on the conveyor belt in a certain way – her way - and if you didn't, her loud raucous voice made you feel stupid. Other customers would turn and look as if there was a problem. Boldly, she went up to the till and lifted the heavy bag of "wul" saying that there were ten bottles. She wouldn't have it and counted for herself, sliding one out to swipe the bar-code. She would not have put it past her to lift them all out and swipe them individually. She placed the blue divider between the school shopping and her own then picked up another to place after her shopping, but instead placed it in her trolley by mistake. Well, the whole of Tesco Extra Large must have heard her. "You've put the shopping divider in your trolley." Unlike her, Joan didn't think it was funny; a serious crime had been committed, God, how could she have been so stupid. That woman needed no excuses. It didn't end there. Her shopping came to £6.03, or so Joan said. She handed her a £10 note and three pennies expecting to get £4 change for Aqua-Fit later, but no. She handed her a fistful of change. "What is this?" she said annoyed. "Well it was £6.05p." " But you didn't say that," she retorted. It was a no-win situation and she stuffed the change into her purse. She could hear Joan telling her friends, if she had any, at break time, about the customer who put the divider in her trolley, as though it was the highlight of her shift. Until then it had been a good day. It was only 7.15 a.m. She set out the vegetables and the pupils had to guess their generic name from the words on the board.

Only seven pupils turned up for the session called "last-minute revision" after school on Wednesday. She had hoped for more. They had said they would come and they had let her down. She was vexed. She had organized a very busy two hours and they would have benefited from the extra input. She ad-libbed the entire lesson, keeping it lively yet focused, darting from one topic to another, the more confident pupils contributing and sharing their knowledge. They talked about coffee shops and take-away lattes. She told them the story of how her take-away latte in a paperboard cup spilt, narrowly missing a lovely dress in the bottom of a carrier bag belonging to the woman sitting opposite on the train. Twice, Linda said "fuck", and each time she reprimanded her telling them all that, never in her life had she said that word. However she did say that she liked the word crap and that she was using it more often. It was a good word. The pupils were in stitches. In front of them she made two dozen blueberry muffins to show the effect of bicarbonate of soda, but also to eat, which they did, immediately calculating that there would be three muffins each.

Bubbling with excitement, the next day, they all piled into her room: Fair Trade had come up in the exam, The Red Tractor Scheme had come up and so had bicarbonate of soda. That was fantastic and well worth doing the lesson for them. If only the others had come too.

In a word, it was wet. For the entire bank holiday weekend wind and rain battered the front of the house relentlessly. In her mind, the sycamore at the front, now as high as the house, had outstayed its welcome. The branches bent and leaned, roaring in the easterly wind. Wet shiny leaves were snatched and hurled to the ground. There were a number of unintentional sycamores in the garden from seeds scattered on the air. Unlike the others, the tree in the front had been allowed to grow. To start with, its insidious growth went unchallenged, but she feared its encroaching roots nearing the foundations. Sometimes the wind eased and the rain fell as drizzle only to gather momentum again.

Clipboard in hand, he honed in on her. Walking up from Monsoon on the way to Marks & Spencers she had seen the young man approach others, looking for a way in. He hardly needed to explain who he was. He was wearing a purple tee shirt with a Great Ormond Street logo across his chest. Showing her the small print on the covenant, he implied that she would not miss a £2-a-week pledge to contribute towards the rebuilding of the hospital, the most renowned and finest in world, caring for the sickest children. It was just a pity that it was so old. He even tried flattery, implying that other people looked miserable and therefore not generous with either their time or their money. She looked around. Yes, they did look miserable. Not taken in by his persistence, pulling her heart strings and pulling at her purse strings, she said no, not that it wasn't a worthy cause, but that she already gave to charities locally in her own high street. Also, committing herself to other charitable events had meant that she was on mailing lists and sent begging letters, especially around Christmas. Enough was enough, not liking the guilty feeling when she left them unopened on the second stair up. She hoped that he wouldn't think her mean and penny-pinching when she walked past him again in half an hour. He hoped that in that time she would reconsider. She crossed the road to Neal Street. Going to Covent Garden had come as a complete surprise about ten past eight that morning when her son realized that she was on half term and that his mother might like to go for a few hours while he was at work. Of course she would, never one to pass an opportunity. Window displays tempted her into the boutiques, and once inside she scanned the rails, looking for interesting fabrics and ideas. There were three things that held her interest and remained in her mind. One, a rigid plastic shopping basket in lime green and orange, real sixties colours that cost a staggering £12. She had been after a basket like that for ages to take swimming. She could see that with a slight squeeze it would fit in the locker instead of a feeble carrier bag. Two, a grey wool second-hand jacket that had the assurance of being dry cleaned and pressed (she thought rather badly). However, she liked the idea of clothes not looking new. Even without trying it on, she knew it would fit and it only cost £20. She had £20 in her purse. And three, the colour red, a worn, faded, red but on a new dress. She sat, having a coffee on the corner of Southampton Street and Maiden Lane to wait for her son. It was an interesting spot with plenty to look at. Something must have reminded her of Mrs Lawrence, a stunning black woman who came into school to do supply. Her first lesson of the day had been art where she herself had been registering the form. She said hello to Mrs Lawrence and said that she liked her outfit. Mrs Lawrence replied that she had made it herself and that she made all her clothes and that she was a textile teacher, and undoubtedly a mistress of her craft. Without hesitation she turned back her wide sleeve, scrutinizing the finish, and touched her arm, feeling the texture while they talked privately about their common interest, next to the paint-splattered sinks, oblivious to the children waiting for the bell. She was good at not spending money and was thankful that she hadn't when her son, at one o'clock, suggested lunch. She had precisely the right change for jacket potatoes filled with curry and a Perroni, times two, sitting under the glass roof of the Apple Market. Wasting time until her son had finished, she went into Waterstones, scanning the fiction section for books by "her" publisher. Systematically she cast her eye along the bottom of the spines, row after row. There was none, and she concluded that the bookshop must be the Tesco of the book world, dealing with only very large orders in order to increase their profit margin.

Once home, she cut the grass. The great weight of cloud of the past few days had slightly lifted and it was warmer.

In the holidays there was a slot at ten o'clock for an hour, before the public swim, for "other" sessions and because she fell into all the options available she could if she wanted, go every day. She tried out her new multi-coloured silicone hat to replace the cheap Sainsbury's bag look. She twisted her hair up and pulled the hat over her head. Without pulling her hair it slipped on comfortably, it had a huge amount of stretch, even over her ears. Under the water, however, she disliked the barking, yappy dog sound and she stopped at the end of her first length to uncover her ears. None of the ten o'clock sessions were busy. She noticed that the man swimming beside her had had his leg amputated from the knee, and when he got out he strapped on his prosthesis and walked away to the changing rooms. The electricians were carrying out maintenance around the pool. It was a father-and-son business. She knew the son part of the business. He used to be in her class about eight years ago. She remembered him being good at practical work.

At last it wasn't raining. The time to do her urgent list of jobs was slipping past. She queued for Aqua-Fit. "Well, it won't be Shaun. I've just seen him with his mum," said the lady in front of her to Dawn behind the glass partition. The ladies loved Shaun, a real mummy's boy. They didn't worry about him being camp, and his harmless, saucy patter got them giggling like schoolgirls. "Any new ladies, put your hands up. Any old ladies, put your hands up." Well, there were plenty of them, but of course being used to Shaun's cheeky innuendo, none of them did. He said it every week and they still laughed. Most of them probably went to the session because he gave them more attention in forty-five minutes than their husbands had given them all week. He was tanned and fit and he made them feel good about themselves. It wasn't Shaun, and the ladies were disappointed. The workout was more forgiving and she too was disappointed. Later, while in the throes of gardening, her friend Wendy called to say that there was a set of Minton china in the window of the RSPCA charity shop in the High Street. As soon as she could be, she was standing in the shop and the assistant was writing a receipt. How could anyone part with such beauty? Well, their loss was her gain. She would collect it in the car the next day. As promised, she did. Each piece had been carefully wrapped in the local newspaper and placed in two boxes. Acquiring such a wealth of china at once was indulgent. She already had a complete set, given to her by her mother over a long time, for birthday and Christmas presents. She herself could never have afforded the outlay until now. It doubled her capacity to serve afternoon tea to twelve people at once and in her creeping old age thought that could be useful. What she needed to do was to buy the cake stand. Once home, she unpacked the boxes, pushing the crumpled newspaper to the bottom of a pink recycling sack and, although she knew that she shouldn't, she loaded the precious Hadden Hall into the dishwasher. The sudden and unexpected addition to her own china was comforting as she delivered it red hot from the machine two hours later. She hoped that the accumulation would not cause problems when she was no longer around and hoped her sons would not dump something that had been so special to her in the local charity shop. Even if she left it to her sons, which one would it be and would their partner/wife/girlfriend like it too? Or would they see it as old fashioned and not want it, or, worse still, treat it badly, putting it in the dishwasher daily, fading the lovely colours, or throw it at the wall because it wasn't theirs in the first place so it didn't matter.

For the entire week, she had been starved of sun. Not a glimmer.

June

Being observed while doing your job was exacting to say the least, especially when twenty children were involved. It was the Indian vegetable curry lesson and she borrowed a sari from her friend. She walked around taking the smallest steps. Somehow she must have gone wrong and tried to remember how to wear it. She played Indian music in the background. She went to all this palaver on special days, and as her CTL was watching her, it was a special day. She arranged the vegetables carefully. The pupils had to name them and decide on the generic name from a list on the board. One girl started badly, calling a cauliflower a cabbage. She had sorted through a whole box to find a piece of ginger that didn't look like a "willy". The pupils didn't need any encouragement. From Wendy she had borrowed a tabor and a machine that could make the special shaped noodles in Bombay Mix, and passed a bowl of it around the class for them to taste. She had a range of spices to show and her many vegetables prepared, sliced and diced ready for the demonstration. The smell of garlic and spices filtered through the extractor system making those on the top floor feel hungry. Taking the folded sari from the drawer in the filing cabinet after school, she handed it to her friend and she showed her again how to deal with the eight meters of fabric. Sarog took hold of the end stamped with the gold writing, letting the rest tumble to the floor, and tucked approximately six inches into the skirt she was wearing around the waist. She continued all the way round, then she folded in short brisk folds a whole wodge of material and tucked that in too, not afraid to show her Indian brown stomach, stretch marks on her navel. The rest of the sari was whizzed up and thrown over her shoulder. It probably took half a minute, not a pin in sight. Of course she remembered. She liked Sarog, she interested her and she made the most divine samosas. She didn't ask if you wanted them, she just brought them in with your name on and the price. Well, of course she paid. They were the sort of thing that she could eat one after the other and unless she put them in the freezer straight away or in the boot of the car where she couldn't reach, they never made it home. If they were behind her seat she would reach behind when she was driving and prise the box open with her left hand and eat them all one after the other. She couldn't help it. Twice, when disaster had struck in the world, Sarog had done her bit. Both for the Tsunami victims and more recently the earthquake victims in China she had made batches and batches of samosas with a dramatic increase in price. Oh, she was shrewd and clever, an opportunist like a crow picking at the McDonald's thrown from the car window into the road, risking all for the reward.

Another woman interested her. She was black and had the most amazing presence. She spoke little English but managed to make herself understood. One minute throwing her washing over a bush to dry in the African sun, next minute trying to get to grips with the timer on the tumble dryer in her room. Her infectious gravelly voice and her wide flashing smile just made her want to know more. As cool as you like, in the middle of a lesson, she would amble into her room, holding an empty disposable plastic cup in her black bony hand. She had come for some washing powder. She took the plastic cup from her and went to the cupboard to fill it. Somehow, it was easier to do that. She hadn't the heart to turn her away, confusing her with bureaucracy. Her tight black wiry hair sprung straight out of her head. It didn't fall over her forehead or press down on her neck making her hot. Her hair had been designed for an equatorial climate. She took it upon herself to find out the interesting woman's name and went along the service corridor to the site team's office. Their corridor and office always looked like a dumping ground and did not reflect the effort that the team made around the school to create a good image. It was tea-stained and splattered and awash with piles of clutter and muddle. The interesting woman was sitting down at one of the desks strewn with pieces of paper. Hovering, she waited for her to look up. When she saw her standing there, the red gash broke across her face, her teeth, white and even, a smooth gold eye-tooth catching the light. She found out that her name was Gina; in case she had misheard she asked her to write it down. No, she had had not misheard but hoped for something more native, and that four years ago she had left Ghana seeking refuge and to escape poverty, and start a different life. The wrench was not without its emotional turmoil. She had left behind her three children. Speaking to them on the phone was no compensation. She found life a struggle, meeting the high cost of living in England and sending money home. She wore black shoes on her broad, cracked feet, her soles dry from years of walking barefoot in rough ochre-coloured soil. Her appearance never gave anything away, always smartly dressed in black with a red corporate image tabard covering over the cracks in the system.

Niru served her at 7.18 a.m. She didn't get her change wrong when she gave her a £10 and 41 pence and received three £2 coins and a £1 coin, even apologizing for the change as she placed it in her hand. On the contrary, she was pleased; she liked the feel of the £2 coins and to be given three at once was good. She slipped them into her purse and picked up the assortment of crisps for taste testing.

They never seemed to have time to talk; break times were non-existent and with good intentions cups of tea were made, but never drunk, left on the side to go cold. At lunchtimes, however, they sat for at least twenty minutes, though still not enough time to talk. They decided to eat out at The Grill so that the three of them could sit and chat and from five until eight. They talked non-stop. Looking around, she was fascinated by the haphazard ambience of the taverna, like that on any Greek island: the random furniture, upholstered dining chairs alongside garden furniture, melamine tables and plastic-coated tablecloths over wooden tables. It was a self-service affair and once the initial welcome was made and the money collected by the grey-haired Greek in the white apron you were left to your own devices to consume as much or as little as you wanted. Traditional Greek music played in the background, capturing a laid-back holiday atmosphere, and on the wall was a picture of Santorini. She could not hear the gentle wash of the wave nor could she hear the donkeys braying and their hooves slipping on the steps. Years ago, she remembered The Grill being a transport café, with a rough clinker frontage onto the Watling Street, and from the outside it still looked much the same.

It was time once again to drive into London and collect her son and his belongings. At precisely 7 a.m. she crossed Waterloo Bridge. Only occasionally had she stopped at traffic lights and had arrived in Cadiz Street sooner than expected. She tapped as lightly as possible on the knocker so as not to wake the others in the house. Within a moment her bleary eyed son was letting her in. The small front room was full of his things, packed and wrapped and ready to load into her car. While her son went to and fro, a man came along sweeping the pavement. He was a big man and quietly proud. He stopped and she said good morning, his broad grin smiled back.

"You leaving?" He said, nodding his head towards the back of the car

"My son is," she replied.

"Where he going?" he wanted to know.

"Near Milton Keynes," she answered.

"What's it like there?"

"Different. Different to here." She continued looking around. "He's been happy here."

They said goodbye and she watched him continue along the street, stopping and brushing as he went.

The brief conversation with the road sweeper had some meaning, unlike the shallow loud exchanges, peppered with coarse language, that carried clearly on the quiet morning air. One of the three white men opposite was unloading a distribution lorry while another watched, hands in his pocket, accepting the goods and signing the delivery note. The other man was nothing to do with the warehouse, he had just stopped by and joined in with the banter, throwing his arms about and having a cigarette. It was harmless.

"You'd talk to anyone, mum."

Fifteen minutes later they were leaving, turning right into Walworth High Street and across the city.

He was going to be born on the 8th. She remembered those spring mornings, lying awake, the birds singing their hearts out in the altering light. Through the open window, she could hear the frenetically charged hum, the incessant twittering, interrupted now and then by the "ark" of the crow and the unmistakable ringing laugh of the woodpecker. From across the field, carried on the still morning air, she could hear the raucous call of Henry the pheasant who lived at Tickford Abbey. He was called Henry by the residents and he would lord it about, fearless of Cat the cat and the tribe of squirrels. Lying on her back, she would spread her hands over her big hard stomach, swollen with pride and her son. Elbows and knees kicked out beneath the tightly stretched skin. She was apprehensive and excited. For her it was a massive step, one that would change her life forever. The 8th slipped past. He was not born on the 8th. Every year at this time she was reminded of her son being born, sitting in the twilight, on the end of the bed feeding him, her husband sound, hoping that she was doing everything right, and, when he cried, feeling guilty, it was all her fault. Maybe he sensed her fear and anxiety, as a dog can sense if people are frightened, or maybe he was plain moody, or maybe it was because he was a Gemini. Whatever the reason for his irritability, she blamed herself.

Between them they didn't have the attention span of a gnat. Not keen on text-speak abbreviations and small-case letters used for titles, she wrote "Learning to Learn" on the board. The pupils knew the phrase as L 2 L. What had they learnt? She asked the pupils in front of her and they told her. She wrote what they said on the board. Within moments into the lesson phones were confiscated and a bin put in front of the boy chewing the gum. Two disruptive pupils were moved. She stood strategically to discourage poor behaviour. They were needy children: misfits who found it difficult to engage with learning and resorted to what they did best, and that was to be naughty. At times they surprised her. Words were thrown up on the board and most contributed; they had learnt that their usual teacher supported West Ham so that went up on the board too, along with the words "visual", "auditory" and "kinaesthetic", and they could tell her what each word meant. They understood too how to mind map and so she asked them to do their own, called "A Sunny Day". If they could remember big words like kinaesthetic surely they could remember the day before. Disappointingly, most had forgotten what they had done the day before. She asked them to read what they had written. They didn't understand that in order to hear they had to be quiet and listen. Then came their task: to design a leaflet explaining to the new intake of year six what L 2 L had meant to them. They folded their sheets of paper in different ways and collected colours from the tray. There was a sigh of relief from most when the bell rang. Maybe they would finish the leaflets next week, maybe they would find their way to the bin. Either way, the pupils would not remember.

The breast screening service had sent a letter inviting her for a routine appointment. She wondered as she sat waiting why they couldn't make homes in a similar way to the self-contained mobile unit. She looked around at the notices and the way the curtain tape had been stitched to the flowery curtains. The nurse called her into one of the four cubicles, where she stripped to the waist. Not wanting to sit exposed and vulnerable, she buttoned her cardigan around her shoulders to wait her turn. The X-ray equipment was not kind to curves and not the most comfortable of positions. Slipping off her cardigan she stood close to the machine while the specialist took her breast in her hands and arranged it against the smooth glass slide. Slowly she compressed a second slide until her breast was sandwiched tightly between, like double-glazing. Instead of averting her eyes, she looked down and saw her shape: deformed, flattened and spread to a thin layer through the glass. It was worse than she imagined, like an exhibit of modern art by Damien Hirst. She should not have looked. Soon it would be over. Her friend Val was in the waiting room. "See you in three years," she called as she left.

However many times she hid the photo in the little oval box, he would take it out again. The photo, passport size, had been taken in a booth when she was young and silly. In spite of being a black-and-white picture, she looked golden and freckly. Her hair, lightened by the sun, was parted on the left and fell over her bare arms. Around her neck she wore a string of red love beads. That picture reminded him of how she was when she was young. How he ached for those times. He might not notice immediately that the picture had gone, but, when he did, he would lift the lid of the oval box and take it out and prop it once again against the mirror.

It was the birthday weekend and it was time to make the requested meatballs. She took the book from the bookshelf and thumbed through until she found the page, well-used and splattered. Familiarizing her mind again with the recipe, she combined the grated onion and cabbage with the mince, then added the spices. In her hands, she took a small amount and rolled it into a ball. When she had used up the mixture, she shallow fried the balls until golden, transferring them to the roasting tins. Then she started on the curry, crushing garlic and slicing the vegetables, neatly ordered on the wooden board. Once the sauce was simmering she poured it over the meatballs and covered the containers tightly with foil. Its pungent spicy smell filled the whole house. They ate outside and washed the food down with icy sangria served from her summery green jug. She had been waiting for just such an opportunity to use it. She made a delicate fluffy meringue, and filled it with copious amounts of thick soft cream and a scattering of raspberries, a deliciously whimsical conclusion to the fiery meatballs.

Drunk and disorderly, her children played cricket and football on the "new" grass, which for the past thirty-five years had been a vegetable garden, rotating crops and providing food. Her son had brought a cricket set with him and excitement rose as it was unpacked. A bail was included in the pack. Within moments the pitch was ready, the stumps positioned and the bail carefully balanced. Her sons made stylish moves, turning the ball and getting spin. Cover was provided by the runner bean canes and square leg by the formidable twenty-foot Leyland Cypress hedge. Jack Russell, alias the upturned wheelbarrow, kept a good wicket as the ball echoed against it. Tiring of cricket, they turned to football, skilfully playing with beer bottles and wine glasses held high in outstretched hands. The "new" grass went to about the end of the garden to the shade of the Bramley apple, under which grass for shade had been sown. She had wanted a stretch of grass to play on and roll around on and sit on, dreamily making daisy chains and love. She invested in a range of balls, half price in Tesco, along with other garden activities, and planned to play badminton and pitch and putt. Already it had brought pleasure and she had seen her husband and son having a kick about, laughing. Of course, the ball went over the fence. It always did. Retrieving it, however, was just as much fun, scrambling over the six-foot fence before they were seen by the neighbours. Their knees were green and their socks filthy because they played in their socks. Out of habit, their trainers had been left at the front door on the mat. It had been hard for her husband to relinquish half the vegetable garden to her grassy plan but since Christmas it had gradually taken shape. She had wanted that feeling of a wide-open space that an empty field gave, to have an uninterrupted view from the kitchen window, to see the sky. She wanted, when she was old, to go for a walk in her own garden and feel a sense of achievement, without others seeing her slow clumsy movements.

"What does frigid mean, Miss?" She had given the two tables towards the back of the room the cold shoulder. Her eyes were fixed and unfriendly. Their general attitude was poor, and their work, low level. The pupils had a vague idea of what it meant and that was how they saw her attitude to them. It was an old-fashioned word and she was surprised that they had even heard of it.

"Someone who doesn't want to get involved; aloof, distant," she replied, feeling rattled, unable to say what her true thoughts on the subject were. And having never needed to know the real meaning, she checked it in the dictionary: "Sexually unresponsive, very cold, excessively formal." They knew what frigid meant.

All week anger had swelled and subsided as she tackled sixty reports and the backlog of marking that had accrued as the result of projects concluding. She so resented giving up her time and would settle to nothing until she had finished, continuing to mark between cooking dinner and doing the ironing. Her target was to complete all by Monday. By Thursday evening, she had made good progress. Then, on Friday morning, she unexpectedly lost her free time to VLE training. Precisely at that moment and time she did not need to know about "virtual" learning. Getting her reports to Dawn was her priority. She was so annoyed at having to endure a whole morning staring at a computer screen. It was her worst nightmare. What made matters worse was that she had to leave her year seven class to the mercy of a supply teacher. Things felt totally beyond her control. Even in the afternoon she was still simmering like the forty saucepans in her room, and when she looked in Sammy's pan and saw the cornflour set like a boulder in the pot of mince she was cross. She spooned out the lumps straight into the nearest bin and asked him to read his recipe and to mix the cornflour again. Such was the commotion that none of the other pupils made the same mistake. She did not listen to his feeble excuses; it was wrong, end of story. She stayed after school until she had finished the reports and gradually her intense frustrations lessened. On Saturday morning there was a knock at the door and she left her marking to answer it. The postman had a parcel for her and she needed to sign for it. It was from the publishers. In the kitchen she sliced through the brown sticky tape with a knife. It was her manuscript to proof read. It now looked like book pages. She was so excited. By 10.15 a.m. everything was marked and packed in her bag for Monday. Free at last, she went for a swim.

There was also a letter from the Breast Screening Unit. "I am pleased to inform you that your mammograms (breast X-rays), showed no sign of breast cancer."

Nothing was still. The whole world was on the move, buffeted and tossed about. Light white cloud streamed in from the south-west, rippled sand, skulls without eyes, feathers and continuous lumps of land, constantly changed, extending and thinning like teased cotton wool, eventually dissolving and disintegrating into soft smudged shapes. Vapour trails stretched into prehistoric spines. Australia swept through twice, softening and falling into the great ocean of sky. Within moments, the cloud cleared in a desperate hurry, only to be replaced with more. When there was a lull, the warmth of high June pressed down. The bamboo wind chime suspended below the pergola was playing at twice the speed. Washing, anchored down with five pegs, flung and flapped around trying to escape in the next gust. Petals were snatched from the roses over the arch and the grass blew away, never reaching the box attached to the mower. She took her scissors from their place in the kitchen and cut a bunch of sweet peas and set their gentle frilly petals in a vase. Perfume drifted invisibly on the air, like scented stocks on a summer evening.

It was Sports Day, the annual event that permitted the wearing of PE kit for the entire day. She sat on a plumped-up cushion overlooking the rounders matches, not liking the idea of sitting directly on the grass, ants crawling over her clothes. Somehow the cushion offered protection. Pupils yelled and screamed encouragement at their teams. She was reminded of her sports days – for her, a test of endurance and ridicule. Not good at sports, especially athletics, she still had to participate. One year on the morning of the dreaded sports day, she took a hammer from the shed and tried to hurt her ankle badly enough to be excused the 200 yards. Deliberately trying to bruise and inflict injury was a hard thing to do and she didn't do that very well either. Another year she was entered for the 800 yards; only four people took part so at the worst she would come fourth and get a point for her house.

It was typical; everything fell on the same day. Arrangements had been made to go out with friends for a meal at Las Iguanas in the Hub, the latest crowded development for socializing in. But it was parents' evening too, and she took clothes to school for all eventualities, changing in the cupboard after parents' evening, into black linen trousers and the high-heeled shoes, not worn since that Thursday lunchtime when she had soaked her feet. Around her neck she wore olives and slices of kiwi, a present from her son on her birthday. Appropriately, they were eating Brazilian.

"Are you going away?"

"Yes I am," she said, indicating the mural of Rio de Janeiro behind their table, the Statue of Christ reaching out over the city and Guanabara Bay.

They sat, exchanging the frustrations of the day, drinking too much, too quickly. Her husband talked about the book he was reading. It was about the terrible times suffered under Stalin, the desperate plight of a country and its peoples and about his family's history and how his grandfather was taken away to Siberia, never to be seen again, no one knowing what became of him. He had a morbid compulsion to find out about his roots and regretted not speaking to his mother before her dementia set in. She would have been able to tell him everything he wanted to know, but he had left it too late. It was a bible of a book and she had heard about it on the radio and made a note of it, buying it for her husband last Christmas. He found it hard going and harrowing and she could tell that it left him feeling like a wrung-out cloth, bitter and consumed with anger. Somehow, the book always came into conversation; the depth of despair felt by the people troubled him. Quietly, she listened. What more could she do? He would even open the book and read a paragraph to her. Thinking about the painful events in the book played on his mind, making him sullen and moody. At times she wished that she had never bought the book in the first place. With that, Zimbabwe came into the conversation, followed by a political rampage on their own government and the cost of just about everything. Surely, there was someone to take a stand and speak up for the ordinary working man in the street, someone to take on board what people were thinking and saying. They thought that the government was very short-sighted about buying oil from Russia. The menacing threat of the Russians having anything to do with the oil supply was unnerving. Thinking nothing of it, they would turn off the supply and let us all freeze to death. They had been just as cruel in the past and they hadn't changed. They were not to be trusted. She redesigned the vegetarian mince for the third day and served it topped with mashed potato and browned in the oven. Confused with drink, her husband didn't notice, or if he did, he didn't comment. Addled by ten, they had had enough of the day.

They took themselves along the familiar towpath, known for over forty years, and in that time the view either side of the canal had barely changed. Usually well trodden, the narrow chalky white path had become overgrown and hidden in places. It was graced with gentle grasses, leaning and swaying, some reached to her shoulders. Smudges of red clover and yellow horseshoe vetch grew everywhere. They walked in single file, her husband in front, setting the pace, much slower than hers. He was wearing shorts and sturdy trainers, his strong legs still brown from last year's sun. She walked in his footsteps. The long grasses brushed his bare skin. Disturbed insects and puffs of pollen rose up. Now and then he stopped, and bent over, scratching where they had irritated. He remembered every inch of that stretch of canal, stopping frequently, seeing the reflection of time mirrored in the brown water, silently remembering endless unspoilt summers.

The pilgrimage to the canal was followed the next day by one to the Oval, to see the start of a game between Surrey and Kent. For her, it didn't quite have the same feel because all the spectators were in a different stand further round the ground, as the match was being played on the furthest wicket. Also, in the toilets there were swanky new Dyson hand-dryers, in her mind, out of character and unexpected. Had the toilets in the other stand had the same make-over? She hoped not. She liked their familiarity. For over thirty years they had always been the same: basic, but clean and airy. They sat in a row of four seats, without the inconvenience of having to let people past, or them bothering anyone else. A few seats behind, a man talked exactly like Harry Dodson, who some years ago presented the Victorian Kitchen Garden on the television. His voice was quiet and soothing, the frequency of the decibels did not change. It was pleasant watching a match without the incessant voices of the commentators and information flashing onto the screen and adverts breaking up the proceedings. She liked the atmosphere of live cricket, a pocket of tranquil calm amid the heaving city. About 1.30 p.m., their son joined them, arriving from the east on his bike and, although not particularly interested in cricket, soon settled into the game, lulled by comforting sounds, the thud of the bat on the ball, the occasional cheer and the murmur of the crowd, the scoreboard opposite slowly changing.

July

Autumn had come early. Something had happened to the horse chestnut trees lining her journey to school. The shining brown sticky buds, which only two months ago were bursting out in all their glory in the spring sunshine, looked dead and dying; their soft green leaves had turned a rusty brown, they were curled and full of holes. The leaf miner moth was causing the damage.

Recently, on Friday mornings about eight o'clock, she and her friend had taken to indulging in a cup of instant coffee, sometimes drunk black when the milk was on the turn. They got their lessons ready then perched on stools, indulging in the pleasure. If for some reason they missed out on the luxury of time, they felt deprived. Her billowy flowery skirt was pulled up, a hint of knee showing. They always had their fair share of visitors, calling in and saying good morning. "It must be summer, Jane is showing her knees." Hastily she pulled down her skirt. Caught off guard, she didn't like to give anyone opportunity to comment.

She stood with another woman on poolside, waiting for the slippery children to finish their lessons, looking forward to feeling the cooling water on her skin. Three trips to the council dump to offload garden waste and hardcore had made her hot. The pool was busy, but above the general noise was the raised voice of a father shouting at his crying daughter. He was trying to teach her to swim and doing it badly. For a moment she watched them. He wore a bluish vest and there was anger and frustration in his eyes and across his face. He held his daughter roughly by the straps of her swimsuit. She was frightened and upset, out of her depth, her hands trying to cling to his close-fitting vest. If he carried on like that in public, what was he like behind his own front door? Really she wanted to intervene, to tell him to leave her to play and get used to the water, to hold her gently and talk to her instead of shouting. As a child, she too was bullied and threatened while learning to swim. She knew how the little girl was feeling and, like her, she would always remember her father's behaviour. What do you do in situations like that? She had felt like that before, wanting to intervene, in the cool air-conditioned papyrus gallery in Cairo. A father, born without arms, for no apparent reason kicked his son in the stomach, knocking him off his feet. He too wore a vest. The memory never left her. He had seemed pleasant enough on the coach, generous and laughing. And when a mother and her children were crossing the High Street in the wrong place and she lashed out at her daughter dithering on the kerb. Why did grown-ups behave like that?

For once it was sunny. It was the day of the carnival, so often a wash-out or cancelled altogether due to the waterlogged field. About one o'clock, she walked with her son to watch the parade. Hearing the music, their step quickened crossing the car park, anxious not to miss the beginning. Just in time, they took up their position in the crowd lining the route. The majorettes were first (well, actually, the police jeep was first), dressed in purple, twirling their batons and shaking their silver pom-poms. Their faces looked as dull as their formation marching, not a smile. The carnival queen and her princesses followed in an open-top car, waving angelically to the minions. Then came the floats, the big scary lorries, highly polished and their horns highly charged, being allowed to drive through the town, but usually banned and cursed if they did. They were decorated for the occasion with banners and balloons. Children waved and played at being grown-ups and grown-ups waved and played at being children. Music played. She and her son threw their loose change into the charity buckets and turned to make their way home. It hadn't lasted long and did not compare to other parades. There was no penny-farthing, no mad clowns, no steel band, no pipe band and the flicking pleats of kilts, the sceptre thrown high in the air. Not surprisingly, over the years, participation had lessened: poor weather, health and safety issues and all the hard work involved organizing such an event, contributing. The crowds subsided. Along the route people had dropped their rubbish: sweet wrappers and screwed up chip papers, left to blow about. Cans and plastic glasses rolled about noisily, gathering momentum until caught and silenced in the gutter.

In the kitchen her son answered the phone and after chatting for a few moments she heard him say, "I'll just get her." She stood up, leaving her tea to go cold. The phone call intruded, taking her away from her immediate thoughts. For that reason she was not keen on phones, mobile phones even less. It was her sister. Along with other well-known sites, the Knolls, not so well known, was a heritage site worth protecting. Her sister had read about it at the weekend in the Sunday papers. At last their mother was on her mind.

"What about scattering Mum's ashes on the Knolls? I presume you still have them in the hall."

"Well no," she replied.

Immediately her sister was stand-offish. Her tone was brusque and businesslike, as though she was talking to one of her patients. She simply said that her ashes had been interred in January, not saying that it was in fact the first time her sister had mentioned the subject in about two years and she had felt left with the burden of it all. Her sister's plan had been foiled. They exchanged pleasantries and updated on the activities of their children. The new kitchen was quite the best yet and with much excavation there was now enough room on the drive for ten cars. In her married life she had had three kitchens: one in her first house, the one left by the people who lived in her house thirty-three years ago, and her present kitchen, built thirty years ago, and apart from a new roller blind and a different colour scheme, it

106

remained the same. The new blind replaced the original that looked old and tired, discoloured and dotted with fading beetroot splashes and flattened moths. She had been cooking beetroot in the pressure cooker when she had heard the steady hiss change. Suddenly the trivet was spinning wildly, whizzing muddy, purple beetroot water across the kitchen. Imagining the trivet launching off, penetrating the ceiling, through the roof of the extension and into space, she picked up the pan and rushed outside with it, where it finally calmed down. The new blind hadn't been established long when she was making gravy one Sunday evening. It was quietly simmering, when all of a sudden it exploded out of the pan. In disbelief she looked in the pan. It was completely empty. The sticky, greasy yellowy contents clung to the ceiling, to the walls and to her brand new blind. Despite the wear and tear she had no desire to change her kitchen and was comfortable with the robust, straightforward room that it was. Her sister, on the other hand, had had many kitchens in her different houses.

"I thought I'd wear green," her sister continued when she enquired about the forthcoming wedding preparations. She took that as a warning. It was very likely that she would have worn green.

It was not like her sister randomly to phone, any more than she would, and the call left her unsettled and feeling discontented. On her way home the next day she called into Homebase and bought a wallpaper-stripping machine. She had been threatening to do so for weeks but had not made it into the car park, preferring instead to go home. Understandable.

Getting the results. Well, she knew he would do it, he had worked so hard. He was focused and planned his time. He abstained from drinking and ate sardines. He did everything right, he deserved nothing less. She was expecting the call about 11.30 a.m., allowing time to get from Euston to South Kensington on the underground. Listed alphabetically, he didn't have to read far down the list pinned to the notice board. She imagined him having a smile from ear to ear. What a fantastic feeling. She was on her hands and knees on the worktop carefully removing a display, each staple prised up with one of her own old vegetable knives purely because the tip of the blade had a slight bend and was perfect. She wanted to rehang the pictures on another wall and didn't want to spoil them. While removing the display a pupil came in to say goodbye and that she would not be back until she collected her exam results in August. Proudly, she told her about her phone call.

"Remember that lesson with the naff cards?" she said from the lofty heights. Being successful is a great feeling. You just can't stop smiling to yourself. "Good luck."

In the evening his achievement was duly recognised when he opened the bottle of champagne. It had been chilling in the fridge since the birthdays, when it had become hidden behind the milk and forgotten.

She took a handful of size two flowerpots from behind the shed and placed them strategically around the new grass and the old grass, estimating the putting shots between. An "England" flag attached to a cane marked the start. Her husband cut carefully around the flowerpots with a trowel using the neat circular turf as a patch, then buried the flowerpot in the hole, flush with the lawn. The course started at the shed, where she planned to keep the scorecards and a mini clip-board with a pencil on a string. Her son made a set of flags out of coloured card and sticky-backed plastic. She wanted the players to take it "seriously". Of course, there was no way that it could be taken seriously, there were too many handicaps. Too much laughing for a start, uneven ground that made the ball unexpectedly stop or change direction; and being intoxicated.

Bored, her son stripped the wallpaper off the bathroom walls with the new machine, exposing the dreadful dry, crumbly, pitted walls. The surface was a mixture of distemper, plaster and what she called the wattle and daub, the original wall. No wonder they needed covering. It looked awful. She spent Sunday smoothing the walls with maroon-coloured medium-grit sandpaper. They would never be really smooth. The air was thick with the fine dust, her hair clogged and matted.

She and her husband took themselves into town to sit outside The Dolphin and watch the world go by. In a daze, she had reached the last day of term, another milestone. As usual it had been hectic and the pressure to get everything done was enormous. But now it was and they sat at a wooden table opposite two Chinese takeaway restaurants and a string of estate agents and could remember the office on the corner always being an estate agent. Her husband had called in, in the autumn of 1972 to find that there were only two houses for sale, such was the demand: a bungalow and a new house, the one they moved into the following February. The High Street was busy with traffic, going home and going out. The warm weather encouraged people to be outside, and where they sat was always busy with people using the nearby cash machine. A slip of a boy, driving a Fiat, pulled in smartly and swerved into a place marked out for disabled drivers, one hand on the steering wheel, the other clasping his phone to his ear. He got out of the car, still with the phone pressed close, talking away for everyone to hear; in his other hand, an open can of Fosters. He sat down with his mates at a table and proceeded to make a roll-up. She and her husband were of the same opinion. Some (her husband called them poseurs) cruised through town in cars with exhausts designed to draw attention to themselves or in cars with aerodynamic spoilers, clipped on like a piece of Airfix, or flashy low bumpers that found it difficult manoeuvring over the speed bumps, slouched low in their seats, one hand on the wheel, the window down and the elbow resting on the door. They drove past, music pumping, trying to look casual and cool in the statutory shades, looking over to see if there was anyone they recognised at the tables scattered across the pavement. It wasn't as though they were anywhere special or there was anyone to impress. Buses pulled in and changed their destination and taxies pulled up and deposited people. Three tractors, their trailers empty, rattled noisily past, indicating right towards Bury Common on their way to collect the hay, cut and baled earlier. They were still sitting when they returned an hour later, weighed down, heavy and labouring, taking it easy over the speed bumps. There was a girl at one of the tables. She had already holidayed, her skin brown with southern sun. She wore denim shorts and a black vest. Around her neck she draped a scarf. Although sitting with a crowd of friends, she was aloof and distant from them. Her laugh didn't appear genuine. She was conscious of her appearance, her short blonde bob clipped back with her sunglasses, the way she sipped the chilled white wine and how she placed the glass back on the table. Maybe she too was a poseuse or maybe was already drunk.

She wore an ill-fitting beige ribbed cardigan and trousers a similar shade. On her bare feet she wore red bootee slippers fastened with Velcro. She sat quietly, her bony working hands in her lap, staring, no longer the strong vibrant woman, the matriarch she remembered, her face etched with turmoil and hardship. Her grey hair, combed back, severely accentuated jaundiced yellow skin, withering and loose over her bones. She had lost the fullness in her face, her features looked different, her nose exaggerated. Her lips disappeared into her mouth. Sadly, her mind had deteriorated, but she still participated in conversation, constantly repeating and instantly forgetting what she had just said. Sometimes her mother-in-law dissolved into her own language and her husband had to translate. But it was the same as she had said in English. Her room was basic, with easy-to-clean furniture that appeared in all the rooms in the home, a single bed, a wardrobe, a set of drawers, a bedside cabinet, a sink and a commode that doubled as a chair. Pictures of her family hung on the walls, in an attempt to keep her alert to what she had. Her husband pulled up the commode to be closer to his mother. Admittedly, it did not look like a commode but she knew that she couldn't have sat on it, and sat down instead on the bed opposite, covered appropriately in the Russian doll print duvet, thankful for once for daytime television that she felt herself glancing at. It was awful that she did because normally she would not be so rude, but knew her mother-in-law would not even notice and she took advantage of that. Cheery people, dressed in spotted blue, stepped into the room with clean washing or asked if they would like a drink. Her husband told his mother that they were going on holiday to South America.

"America," she said, picking up the last word in the sentence.

Triggered suddenly, as though it was yesterday, breaking free of her troubled mind, fiercely, she spoke of the isolated image appearing. The Germans came to her village and rounded up people, leaving her mother. She was taken in the night and herded with them like a frightened animal, awash with terror and fear, onto a truck and then a train, packed tightly and left to stand for the entire journey to north Germany. People died on the way and were simply thrown off the train. How her husband's grandmother must have wept for her daughter. A picture, albeit a photocopy, sat on the bedside cabinet. It was of his grandmother and his uncle with his wife and daughter taken during the fifties. His mother had rubbed and rubbed at her mother's face, obliterating it from the original photograph. Was touching her face the only way of being close or did she hate her or simply not know what she was doing? Not surprisingly, unsmiling faces stared back blankly, drained of emotion. She muttered and cursed her own children, who she claimed, failed to visit. She was scathing and irrational about them. She felt sorry for her sitting there day after day. It was no life, waiting to die, struggling with a tangle of jumbled memories and she preferred to remember her with her sleeves rolled up scrubbing her grandchildren in the bath until they shone.

The yellow lacy "balcony bra" displayed on a mannequin beside the till was tempting. Did it imply that it was a holiday essential worn while sitting on the hotel balcony or that it gave an uplifting shape? Piles of clothes had been accumulating for a few days. Things were added or removed until the desired weight was achieved on the fishing scales and she was glad when the bags were finally zipped up. Getting ready to go on holiday was like Christmas. Right until the last minute there seemed to be something else to buy, something that they couldn't be without. Taking herself to Bicester Village she hoped to pick up a bargain. She didn't particularly like the place and maybe went once a year. It was not real; it was like a model village, or a toytown, or a stage set for a film, or even an animation. She also went to Marks & Spencer, which was a matter of course, and last but not least to Boots the chemist for the very necessary insect repellents and sun lotions. At last they were on their way. Her son had generously given up his time to transport them to the airport, removing the tension of the Sunday afternoon traffic congestion and finding a place in the fields of glinting dusty cars, the long-stay car park. To her, getting out of England was the worst part of the journey. Waiting at Heathrow on that quiet pink evening she and her husband watched the planes landing and taking off until it was their turn. It was to be a very different holiday, not really a holiday at all, more of an experience, visiting four different places in less than a fortnight and travelling thousands of miles between each. Originally it had been just a trip to Rio de Janeiro, but the excitement of being so near the rainforest was hard to resist, as were the falls at Iguacu, which they had seen on television during the winter, and to be so near Salvador and not see the old colonial buildings and the beaches of white sand and feathery palm trees – they couldn't miss that - and besides, they needed a couple of days to wind down.

Rodrigo met them at the airport in Rio de Janerio, waiting at Arrivals with her husband's name boldly printed on A4 paper.

August

Caught up in the early-morning rush hour the journey into Rio was slow. Vultures spiralled overhead, the roads were grubby and unkempt. They passed the poverty of the shanty towns. She was glad that she hadn't gone to the bother of washing her skirts before packing them. Seeing through sleepless eyes, she felt apprehensive. Rodrigo chatted away, telling them this and that. Forgetting that it was only 9 a.m., they ordered a beer and took in the views from the roof of their hotel overlooking Copacabana. Spectacular. Sleep. Refreshed, they went out and walked along the wide wavy pavement beside Avenue Atlantica, waves rolling in and crashing on the beach. They visited the statue of Christ the Redeemer at the top of Corcovado Hill, the "must see", his arms outstretched over "his" people. From there, the gently rocking cable car ride to the top of Sugar Loaf Mountain was next. How could a small cloud in the midst of a blue sky insist on hugging the summit? But it did. It seemed to exude from the mountain itself, preventing them seeing the dramatic view. They spent some time on the beach. She stood in the bubbling foam longing to go in, watching the waves, timing them, daring herself. But the waves broke in a fury, rolling, big and dark like those in the old

"Old Spice" advert. If only she could get to the other side of the breaking wave, into the calmer rolling swell. But the pull was too great, even around her ankles, the wave would have had her over, tumbling and falling, gulping and swallowing. She needed the strength of her sons, to encourage and take her hand as she had done for them when they were small. "Rio by Night" was on the itinerary. Visitors were collected on the Grey Line bus from various hotels around the resort and taken to a big airy restaurant that served severe amounts of carne, slivered wafer thin at the table in front of you, from skewers two feet long. Following that they were treated to a musical extravaganza of Brazilian music and dance in an old colonial building. The vibrant energy concluded with the carnival atmosphere spilling into audience participation, and she was glad to be sitting two rows back.

The driver pulled hard on the phlegm lodged at the back of his throat. It was disgusting. The car moved like a streaming ribbon through the morning traffic to the airport, leaving the city and the crumbling shabby shanty towns behind. They were bound for the lush green of Iguacu and met by William, holding a sheet of A4 paper with her husband's name on it. Seeing the Iguacu Falls was breathtaking; nothing on the television had prepared her for the sight. All around, a streaming fichu, gathered and ruched, hugged the neck of the land, glittering and dazzling with millions and millions of tiny bubbles descending and plunging into a mass of frothy petticoats. The almighty, thundering, unrelenting noise of so many waterfalls in one place was awesome, culminating at the "Garganta do Diabo", where there was a tightness in the rocks, where the avalanche of water screamed, foaming and roaring over the precipice, the torrential force plunging into the depths, its immense power forming dense clouds of spray and a veil of mist that rose in the afternoon sky. Swallows darted behind the sheering sparkling torrent to their nests. Footpaths had been built so that visitors could experience the savage force of the cascading water. Oxygenated and energized, the river below flowed at a furious pace. Everything was drenched. The whole place was exhilarating, totally mesmerizing. On the Argentinian side of the falls the next day, a walkway took them over a wide expanse of river. The dramatic views were amazing. Every turn was a photo opportunity. William advised a lunch on the Argentinian side of the falls, It was nothing short of a meat feast and she consumed the equivalent of a family joint washed down with a local beer. Indigenous people sat cross-legged, hoping to sell their crafts displayed on a blanket on the ground. Her husband insisted on buying a painted wooden toucan. The money for the toucan was a drop in the ocean, the people were so poor. They saw a fish eagle catch a fish and carry it in his claw to a rock where he proceeded to devour it. They saw a jewel of a humming bird, splashing in the quietness of a water fountain. They saw a cayman, basking in the shallows. The Parque das Aves aviaries were a fanfare of colour, just pure brilliant extravagance, no-expense-spared plumage, scarlet ibis, toucans, macaws and parrots, all rallying for equatorial celebratory status.

Very early the next day, William took them to the airport, bound for Manaus and the Amazon Village.

She had never really visualized such a city in the middle of the forest, but then this holiday was continually opening her eyes. The expanse of the river Negro was as wide as she could see and that, they say, is twenty-two miles. She had never seen a river so wide. Even seeing it from the air as they were coming into land was spectacular. A thin band of green fringed the curve on the far side. It was busy with every type of boat. Ocean-going container ships dropped anchor at Manaus and one-man canoes paddled past. Francesco had met them with the now-familiar piece of paper at arrivals. He came in a bus, just for the two of them, apologizing for the transport but that the car needed attention. He was friendly, as indeed all the guides and drivers were. He dropped them off for a twenty-four hour stop at the Tropical Hotel, situated on the banks of the river, before being taken by boat to the Amazon Village on the Puraquequara Lake. It was intensely hot, blisteringly hot. To escape the welding white light, they sat on the wall in the shade, overlooking the river. They were happy with that. They watched the smaller boats come into a small jetty and pick up the local people who had been to market. They loaded their plastic tubs of unsold goods onto the boat, then threw up their hammocks in the shade of the canopy, gently rocking until heat and tiredness silenced. It was to be their last day of comfort and luxury for a few days and they indulged in having lunch in the airy foyer bar, watching all the comings and goings of the busy hotel. Marco met them and along with others they went by minibus to the port, a chaotic junction, a meeting of civilisations. A market lined the busy road, sparkling fish lay side-by-side and exotic and unfamiliar fruits were piled high on the rickety wooden stalls. Brown children played and splashed in the river between the ferries. Leaving the frenzy of the port they headed downstream, past the Encontro das Águas where the Rio Negro and Rio Solimöes meet, a truly powerful sight. It was at this point that the river was called the Amazon. Their wooden, palm-roofed lodge hidden amongst the trees and creepers, was number thirty-five, and their welcome pack included a box of matches for the candles. There was electricity, run off a battery, but it was barely adequate in the wooden darkness and they were advised only to use it at night when it was really dark - and it was really dark, black dark, can't-see-a-thing-dark. She didn't sleep a wink on the first night. Of course, the smouldering black Brazilian coffee hadn't helped. They had been out on the river, under the dark starry sky, cayman spotting, and returned to the bar for a drink and a game of dominoes. They opened the door of their lodge and automatically reached for the light switch. Even in the dimness of the light they saw the most enormous beetle on her husband's bed. So far, she had gone to bed scantily clad, but now it was time for the pyjamas and the socks and, had she had one, a woolly hat, too. Even the thought of something crawling over her bare skin made her uneasy. In the dining room that evening there had been frightened screams and a great scraping of chairs, heavy chairs made out of real wood, when the most enormous hairy-legged spider, a tarantula as big as her hand, crawled up the back of a chair. They then overheared a cynical remark from one of the guides, who calmly stood up to see what all the commotion was about. "Welcome to the jungle." She tied her long hair up in its usual fashion for bed and lay down on her side, facing her husband, her knees drawn up and her hands between her thighs, beneath the blue cotton sheet. The wafer-thin, blue and white stripy pillow was mean, and she moved it away from the wall, just in case something crawled up the back of the bed and amongst her hair. It was humid and far too hot. It was airless and still. She dripped with sweat and could feel rivulets gathering into beads of water. Where her neck rested, the pillow was wet, her pyjamas too were soaked with perspiration. The night was long. She lay, wide awake, with her eyes shut, in the same position for the entire night, not daring to move, cast, only her mind alert to the beetles and spiders that lurked in dark corners, that dropped like stones from the raw palm roof onto the bare wooden floor. She couldn't even say that she was frightened, because she wasn't. Gradually, as dawn broke, so the vibrating orchestra of the jungle increased to such a pitch that she was glad to get up. Throughout her wakeful night there had been ticking, buzzing, humming, chirruping, all singing and dancing in perfect harmony with the occasional crescendo, a screech or a call from an animal or the sound of paws in dry leaves or birds landing on the roof. But in the morning the high frequency chainsaw sound from the beetles joined in, and, with that, the humans got up. Each lodge had a basic bathroom and she was thankful to shower in its cool, silky softness. Advised to cover up for the jungle trek, she laced up her boots and wore her hat. The guides were brilliant and drew attention to so many things that, to the layman, would have gone unseen. They showed how the indigenous peoples would use the forest and make use of the different trees, for antiseptic and fire and food and materials for building, and ropes and quinine and inhaler to clear a blocked nose; and how to climb the tallest trees to escape the jaguar and how, by rubbing an ant's nest onto skin it would get rid of human smell, and how to fish for velvety tarantulas with a live fly - handy tips that you need to know in the jungle. After lunch they went out on the canoes to visit the natives in the local villages. They were so poor. Compared with her, they had nothing, nothing more than what they had around them, gleaned from the forest. They made simple jewellery out of wood and pods and seeds and sold it to the tourists. One family kept a boa-constrictor to keep down the vermin. They had a gentle sloth as a pet. They squeezed sugar cane through a mangle made of wood, and scrawny chickens ran around pecking in the dirt. There were several children lined up quietly at the table where the crafts were displayed, watching the white people. She would never know what they were thinking. The next village was more affluent: some houses were made of brick and she could hear music coming from one. They had a meeting room with a pool table and the jewellery was more expensive. A mother was washing up in the lake, and her baby, swimming beside her, was wearing inflated arm-bands. Another world. They spent the next day with the Dutch couple, Alexander and Miranda, and in the morning went piranha fishing in the mangrove, each of them thrashing the water like mad with the end of their rods, a thin branch tied with a length of line and a hook. Marco gave them a handful of cubed meat for the bait. It was fast and furious and good fun. Prepared on a paddle, the fish was cooked and served to them at lunchtime. Returning, a pink-nosed dolphin surfaced. In the afternoon they went canoeing in the mysterious, oily calm of the mangrove, quietly paddling, floating and drifting amongst the eerie trees and roots mirrored in the water, sunlight trying to penetrate, casting silent shadows and pools of dappled light. Getting used to her surroundings, she went swimming off the jetty in the warm tea-coloured waters of the lake. It was time to leave and she waited for the boat to take them back to Manaus, gently swinging in the hammock on their veranda. Her husband settled up; they had had nineteen beers and three bottles of mineral water. Surely the wrong way round.

It was a long day waiting at airports and flying to Salvador, met by Carlos and delivered to their hotel and the all-important ocean view. The bed was four pillows wide with white sheets turned down. Her husband thought it was his lucky day: the room had several lights and the air-conditioning blew. Below, the ocean crashed onto the rocks. Bliss. How they slept. Salvador was different and she expected it to be so. The sand was pale but the sea refused to let her in and she had to be content to watch its energy thundering in, breaking over the rocks and washing over the beach, frothing and foaming, darkening the sand as it ebbed. The beach bar was informal. They sat and read, their feet in the sand, watching the sea, having a beer. It was easy. People were loose-limbed and relaxed. Carlos was available as a guide and saw them as an opportunity too good to miss. He took them out at one o'clock in his air-conditioned car and showed them the sights and explained the history. He warned of beggars and there were. People pestered for money. A pregnant girl held up her top, exposing her big brown belly, holding out her hand, and two very insistent children tried their luck, without success. They walked the narrow cobbled streets of Pelourinho, the old town that opened onto airy squares, where once there had been impressive old buildings, sadly demolished to make way for the car. Dogs and cats belonging to no one, lay, looking dead on the pavements, the heat sapping their energy until the evening when they prowled and roamed. The old town was what she had in her mind. She took photos, like the ones in her guide book, of the old colonial houses, painted in soft pastel shades, but they were pale and shabby in comparison and the light was different. Those in the book were bathed in a golden morning glow. They visited the Catedral Basilica, much of it ornately carved in wood and covered in gold leaf. They walked the peaceful cloisters of Igreja e Convento de São Francisco, each tiled picture including a moral, and visited the church, opulent and lavishly decorated, again in gold leaf. Signs of Africa were everywhere, an inheritance of the slave trade. From a street vendor, a Baiana woman wearing the traditional white lace dress, her head wrapped in a turban, she bought acarajé, a ball of mashed black-eyed beans deep fried in palm oil, then split and filled with shrimps, okra stew and hot sauce, wrapped in a piece of paper, which she ate on the move. The taste of palm oil lasted all afternoon and the smell lingered on her hands. Carlos had filled their heads with history and geography, religion and politics. He had shown them the architecture and pointed out the sculptures, the lighthouses, the Baroque churches, the port, and the malls, where people loved to shop. Like Rodrigo, William and Marco, he knew about everything, explaining in perfect English, promoting Brazil, proud to be Brazilian. They were great. Not knowing, she had underestimated the warmth of the people and the vastness of the country and what it had to offer. It had been amazing.

They lingered over breakfast, not wanting it to end, watching the fishermen in their rowing boats throwing their nets over the side into the heaving sea. It was their last day before reality returned. Understandably, she was quiet, pensive, even. After two days, they no longer paid attention to the rough broken pavements, the dog shit and the rubbish tipped onto the street. This was how it was. They spent most of the day on the beach, moving their plastic chairs in and out of the shade of the umbrella, and, like others, having a beer, watching the world go by. Carlos

119

saw them safely to the airport. Hearing "Good morning" on the BA flight to São Paulo, pulled them up sharp. It was the end of the holiday.

Her manuscript was there on her return, along with the cover idea. There was not time to dwell on the strange feeling of being home, at a loss. By Wednesday it had been proof-read and returned. The cover, however, she was not entirely happy with. It needed to have more impact, to be bolder. She wanted it to be tactile, for people to want to pick it up and hold it. She wanted their eye to be drawn. She wanted it to stand out from all the other books on the shelf. It was unique. She didn't want to hurt anyone's feelings; they might have thought they had done a good job on the cover. She phoned Cheryl, and by Friday a new cover had been produced. She signed her approval and posted it off.

That night her room hung with creepers.

Catching up with friends. Having the time, she pulled on her brakes and crossed the road, stopping her bike beside Lesley her friend, walking as usual, in a tearing hurry, pulling the shopping trolley behind her. Usually buoyant, despite everything in her world unstable, she could tell she looked sad. Her eyes didn't light up; something was bothering her. They shared their news and as usual hers wasn't anything to smile about. Her three sons were never without their problems and their mother was always there to sort things out and pick up the pieces; put upon. "They just don't work at it. They give up at the first problem." Clearly she was irritated by their lack of commitment, then came the real reason for her quiet mood. Her grandchildren, who had been temporarily living at her house, had moved out, and, understandably, she was missing them, the house no longer filled with laughter and squabbles. Her friend was such a good person. She was caring and kind and she was sorry that her sons were so thoughtless. Could they not see that their mother too needed love and attention. Leaving the bank, she met Janine, also enjoying the holidays, with time to talk. They talked about living and dying and dreams. Janine was adamant that dreams were an intrinsic part of life. There was a lot of truth in what she said. Digging deep into the nitty-gritty of her own past, it was all there: memories muddled up with the dreams, muddled up with the here and now and the gone for ever, a tangle of chips and wires, stored and kept on file waiting to be downloaded in the middle of the night.

Later, while busy in the front garden, Wendy, walking her dog Daisy, crossed the road to talk and catch up with the news. They stood in the middle of the uncut grass, her in her yellow rubber gloves, hands on her hips, her friend controlling her inquisitive dog. They talked about their headaches that came and went at the end of term and a pain that they felt in their ears, and she recalled the strange feeling in her ears when she was swimming and kept stopping to rub them. They feared the worst. It was just end-of-term tiredness, the batteries low. Listening to grown-ups talk - and how they could talk – was boring for dogs, and Daisy sat down. They talked about Indian food and Indian clothes and, of course, Brazil. Wendy's pretty glass necklace matched the stripy top exactly. Rain threatened, her friend continued her walk, and she cut the grass before it did.

While they had been away, her son had made a start on dismantling the drive and she went to the dump to offload the rubble that was accumulating in a rocky pile. She felt disappointed that there was a need for such a place, employing at least ten people full time, operating twelve hours a day. Rubbish was expensive. It was, indeed, a "throw-away society". She parked the car at the hardcore container. Besides rough subsoil and old plaster, there were toilets and bricks that had never been used, tiles and slates. To be honest, the waste was awful. Some people, like those who lived in villages on the banks of the Amazon, didn't even have a toilet, or a sewage system, or even running water, yet there in the skip was a gleaming white toilet that was gradually being smashed to smithereens. A man took a perfectly good bike out of the boot of his car and, holding it by the frame, threw it over the wall amongst all the other flotsam and jetsam. She was no better, caught up in the culture of changing and improving, not satisfied with what she had. The rough old drive, cracked and crumbly, was at least forty years old and had been dug up for new pipes and repaired several times. She longed to pull in onto the smooth clean lines of a block-paved drive. Clearing the concrete was a massive job and she enlisted her son to break it up with a pick and a mallet, while she went backwards and forwards to the dump with it all, carefully wedged in her small car.

She could not believe that in two weeks' time she would be trying to teach Adam again. Towards the end of term she had briefly scanned the timetable, not wanting it to be a complete shock on September 1st. Instead of Friday afternoons, she would see him on Monday mornings. On and off, these terrible thoughts were looming in her mind, and, worse than that, she could not believe it was going to be September. Already, there was an autumnal feel in the air. Already, it was dark when she left Aqua-Fit at nine o'clock. Fear and dread.

A rip of light fell across the wardrobe opposite. It was still not time to get up and she lay between a warm drowsy sleep and her mind fighting back, thinking, going over the past two weeks, thinking about what she had achieved. Not enough. She had done some things. She had gardened and cooked and baked and filled the house with friendly smells. She had gathered blackberries and dug dreamy white potatoes. She had chosen wallpaper for the bathroom and taken her glasses to be mended and she had been to the pool. Her children had come for meals and popped in and out because she was at home. So the time drifted by. Purposely she had got up as normal, around six, hoping that the extension to her day would make the holiday seem longer. She avoided using the car and didn't wear her watch, trying to keep things quiet and low key in an effort to slow time down – not wanting to feel the pressure of term time. She began thinking about her trip to Glasgow and the West Coast with her son, planned for the following week. She had not before been to either and the possibility of going to Glasgow and back in a day had been scuppered when the cost of £200 failed to impress. They would go in the car and had started checking the route in the atlas. Occasionally, a car passed and she could clearly hear the woodpecker tapping. Gradually, the light changed and her room reappeared. She got up and wrote a "to-do" list, including on it obvious things that she would do anyway, but see a sense of achievement when she gave herself a tick for doing it.

Unexpectedly, she met up with her two daft friends. There was a time limit. Just as well. All three of them had arrived separately but parked in the same car park where the limit was two hours. They could have talked all day but after two cups of coffee and a glass of wine they pulled themselves away, only to continue in the car park, keeping an eye out for the traffic warden.

She could see that the letter on the table had been franked at school and she picked it up, assuming it to be a standard letter sent to all staff about the recent exams. It was indeed a standard letter but not about the exams. It was sad news about a pupil who had had an anaphylactic reaction to a bee sting and died. Later in the day, she was in the garden enjoying patches of blue sky between the clouds and could hear the phone in the kitchen ringing. She levered herself from the chair. It would be one of her sons wondering if there was dinner. It came as a shock, the second in a day. Her friend had given up her "Race for Life". She had seen her last on the first day of spring, positive and getting stronger. Her friend's daughter was phoning to let her know that her mother had died in her sleep. Her friend was no age, in her forties, always reading and learning, calm as a windless summer's day. She remembered her lethargy and her calmness infuriating when she was an employee of hers, taken on as a school leaver to learn how to sew. "Oh well," she would say if she hadn't finished sewing on the twenty covered buttons down the back of a dress. Being naïve and innocent in the business world she didn't remember telling her off, but finished sewing them on herself when she had gone home. In recent years, her friend practised Reiki and had amazing healing powers. She usually had a session in September and that set her up for the year ahead. It energized and relaxed, it sorted and balanced. Nasty thoughts about horrible kids were banished. She would miss her not being around, quietly getting along in the next village. She would miss her not being there to calm and smooth out her life. She could see that she would not be around for the service on Friday and that bothered her.

She blamed her mother's fond memories for her desire to visit the West Coast of Scotland and remembered her reciting poems and singing traditional Scottish songs (which she would have learnt by heart as a child) and telling the story of being caught in a storm between Oban and Mull, the waves washing over the boat and baling out, lucky not to have drowned. She would stumble and laugh and be vexed if she grazed her bare legs against granite or worse, ladder her stockings. Her mother knew the Highlands and islands and walked, her thick legs in her stout shoes. She would laugh out loud in the big wide space. She had been as far west as Helensburgh and as far north as Ardlui at the end of Loch Lomond when she went with her husband in their teens on a day trip from St Andrews. It was not unusual to down tools and go away with her son. He had nothing much on his agenda until October and welcomed the change of scenery, which indeed it was. The freedom of the car allowed them to change their minds about Glasgow, preferring instead to head for the country, and by twelve they were at Luss, paddling in the cool still waters of Loch Lomond. After a five o'clock start they had only stopped twice, once at the toll booth to pay for the privilege of using a completely empty road (in her mind, worth every penny) and once for petrol where they stretched their legs, used the facilities and ate their robust breakfast of coronation chicken sandwiches. Drizzle around Penrith spoilt her best-loved part of the motorway. It was a favourite part, where the land heaved up out of the earth. Big and strong. Tucking in behind a lorry in the slow lane, she was unable to see a thing, apart from the lorry, that is. Besides talking, they entertained themselves with Radio 4 and especially selected CDs from her son's extensive repertoire. At 5.20 a.m. they started with the shipping forecast, which, so vital to many living and working around the coast, was amusing to her son, who had never heard it before. Later, in business news, the gloomy state of the economy was compared to Table Mountain and Everest. Even listening to serious news could be humorous. They listened to Johnny Cash and the Doors and snacked on bananas and apples. The journey through Glen Coe to Fort William was vast, a remote wilderness, extreme, mist and cloud sweeping in, pylons striding out across the land, heather hugging the ground, carpeting great pink swathes. She was sure that there would be deer submerged in the dark depths of trees, standing perfectly still, watching and listening, just as there would be eagles, perched high, slowly turning their heads, surveying. It was eagle country; she could tell. Parking the car at the foot of Ben Nevis, they changed into walking boots and checked the weather forecasting stone at the stile. It was barely moving. All the way up, water seeped and trickled out of fissures and cracks in the mountain, pouring and gushing, spewing out in torrents. It was a wonderful walk, hard work for her, exhilarating. The wind whipped at her hair, stinging her face, cloud shrouded. As they neared the top, driving mist and drizzle soaked her trousers, her hair dripped and she longed to blow her nose, her only tissues totally inadequate for the conditions. As many others had done, they placed their stones on the cairn. The wind picked up and the drama continued when a Royal Navy helicopter slowly approached around the side of the mountain, suspended menacingly, the noise of the rotating blades deafening. Compared with climbing up, they seemed to fall down the mountain, leaping streams and gathering speed. Her legs were like jelly and she collapsed in the car. How her legs would ache in the morning. Her hands were still cold when she tried to sign her name in the visitors' book at Ben View. "Did you no have yer gloves on?" Sheila (they called the landlady Sheila) made her feel ill-prepared for the assault on "The Ben" and to think that she wasn't going to wear her jacket. How irresponsible, thinking that she could climb the highest mountain in Britain in nothing more than her little pink cardigan, appearing totally unprepared for the inclement weather that could occur within moments. That was far worse than not wearing gloves. She ate Cullen Skink and her son ate haggis, neeps and tatties. Unlike the cold, business- like reception from Sheila, they sank into the warm flowery room glad to be accommodated. Although the pressure to have one was great, she didn't own a mobile phone, so her son sent a message to his father on his, all in lower case: "hello have been up ben nevis x". The reply came back: "ive been up the garden x". The window was open and the curtains moved gently in the damp air. Pushing away the great wall of duvet she lay awake, listening to the different night sounds filtering in, aware of the rain pattering on the window and cars travelling south through the night, their tyres hissing on the wet road. She liked to think that she heard a nightjar out on the moor, although it was more likely to be a tawny owl. Dreaming.

They left early to catch the train across Rannoch Moor and could not refuse the cheery man with the tea trolley, who insisted that they had a drink. They were glad that they did when the not-very-hospitable man, an Englishman, at the only place to go near Rannoch Station, refused them breakfast, saying that they had finished cooking. It was only nine o'clock. They hurled abuse to the wind as they walked off down the road, breakfasting later in the tea-rooms at the station, perched on a stool overlooking the loch. "Sure by Tummel and Loch Rannoch and Lochaber I will go".

It was a wild and hostile place, desolate and haunting. Mist scrolled across the moody sullen sky. Tourist information warned of treacherous mires and not to venture from the path. Plants were low, out of the wind, gripping the ground. Pockets of bell heather and clumps of ling stood firm in the tufts of coarse grass, along with the bobbing blue heads of devil's bit scabious and the yellow lesser spearwort, softening the harsh reality. The bare black bones of trees lay where they had fallen a long time ago. The untamed, forbidding landscape had a moody atmosphere and was probably best left to the finches that swooped about, happy enough.

As she knew they would, her legs were beginning to ache, her arms too, from holding the steering wheel for nearly nine hours. It was a pity it wasn't the "bingo arm" muscle that had been exercised.

Returning to Fort William, they set off for Skye via Kyle of Lochalsh, past shimmering lochs and mile after mile of stunning mountains where the fragmented land reached into the sea. They planned to be brave and swim. Her son checked the beaches in the road atlas that was beginning to fall open on the page called the Western Isles. Cattle and sheep littered the eleven miles of single-track road to Talisker Bay, and after half an hour of walking they were disappointed. Black sand. It was so lonely, desperately lonely. Slowly they made their way back to the main road and north to Uig, past the brooding shoulders of the Cuillins. In the distance it was lighter and brighter with a promise in the sky.

Claire, her real name, showed her the room. It was so Scottish and artistic and overlooked the bay. A fat bundle of cherry-red towels sat on each side of the bed, a little bar of glycerine soap on top. She recommended two places to eat and they chose the one in the harbour. They ate local haddock and drank Blaven, a local beer, named after one of the Cuillin Hills. Midges bit as they walked back. Her son found the Wee Book of Scotland on the bookshelf in the toilet and proceeded to dip in and out of it telling her facts. He sent a message to his father: "hello, staying in uig on skye. night night x", and the reply, "im watchin forest on sky but I cant c u good night x". Known as the Coral Beach, cattle walked along the white sand that curved round the bay. Bracelets of shells edged the gently lapping sea. Bending forward they collected. Not having her glasses, she chose shells that looked like sweet corn kernels. Bravely, her son swam, swimming through bladder-wrack and long ribbons of kelp. Although disappointed in herself for not doing so, she knew that she would not like the feel of the slippery greeny brown tendrils wrapping around her arms and legs, holding her down. It looked as though there could be seals, and she kept watching the water for bobbing heads. She felt sure that there would be seals. They made their way to Armadale, past the low thatched cottage weighted down with boulders tied with rope, to catch the Caledonian Macbrayne ferry to Malliag. Arriving early, there was time for fish and chips at The Shed. They waited patiently in the queue. She pulled forward, never entirely sure of the metal seam overlapping the land, and wondering how the ferry didn't mysteriously float away. The man in the "high-vis" jacket beckoned: come forward, come forward, his arms dancing and swooping. To the left, to the left, a bit more, a bit more; then the palm of his hand up smartly: stop, within an inch of the car in front. They stood for the short journey on the open deck, her eyes scanned the sea watching for seals and dolphins. Back on the mainland, on the Road to the Isles, they drove back to Fort William then south to Oban, listening to Madam Butterfly. Seeing the red long-pile carpet on the stair when the man opened the door, she shuddered. It was only a carpet, she repeated to herself, uncertain of how room number seven would be. It was light and flowery; she could cope with that. When the man had gone, she untucked her duvet and smelled the covers. Everything was as it should be in the bathroom. It was fine. They ate local mussels and scallops with Stornaway black pudding and Aberdeen Angus Steak, and Gaelic coffee to finish. There was not enough time. Oban had been an add-on, a break in the long journey home. They really only had time to walk around the harbour and take some photos. After breakfast, they drove along the coast to Ganavan Bay. The air was warm, not a breath of wind to ripple the sea or blow gently on wet skin. There was not a murmur from the waves, not a sign of seaweed. The sand was white. It was her turn to muster up the courage and she walked straight in. Yes, it was cold but not life threateningly so; it did not grip like a vice or turn like a corkscrew. She did not turn blue. Having been so brave the day before, her son, still warm with sleep and warm with breakfast, was not so willing, and she was out and wrapped in a towel before he took the plunge. It was a lovely end to their trip. She had lost count of the lochs, calm and deep in thought, reflecting the sky, mountains mirrored in the still, glass-cold water. Their journey took them past a village called Rest-and-be-Thankful. If only they could. They took the long lumpy, bumpy road beside the banks of Loch Long towards Glasgow and the south, listening to Mogwai, Tom Waits and Bob Dylan. If only there was more time. They progressed well and stopped around Gretna Green for petrol and a coffee, glad to spend the foreign currency in her purse. As they reached the industrial north, they slowly ground to a halt, then edged slowly forward for miles and miles.

The last day of the holidays was drab. The sky was drab and a thick cloud of dread and foreboding settled over her. All day the impending start of term crept in and out of her thoughts, shutting out her sun, intruding. She lacked spirit and optimism, which was unlike her.

September

At the time she felt that she had achieved very little; the days had no shape. Indifferent to the meetings, she launched into being creative with the displays and resources, and by Wednesday her room was looking good, and by Friday she was back in full flight.

She hadn't been to the health centre for years and the procedure had changed since she was last there. First, she needed to get past the guards on the desk. They wanted to know her inside leg measurement before securing an appointment with the doctor. She was hardly a frequent visitor to the place. She could so easily have not bothered, just turned around and walked home again. She had had her ailments for years but not got round to doing something about them. For her, walking into the health centre was a real achievement, and making the appointment a positive step forward.

"May I ask what it's for?" She wasn't going to say about her rugby player's itch, her toes and her twisted spine. What business was it of theirs anyway?

"Well, what do I need to have to see the doctor?" she insisted.

He called her name and she stood up. They exchanged pleasantries. Yes, she was well. Immediately the order in her mind went out of the window and the toes were first. He said that her toenails had a fungal infection and looked disgusting and that they were trying to imitate ram's horns and would take up to a year to improve. The very words fungal infection conjured up a picture of a nasty, insidious, acrid, poison in an evil yellow. Also, they were lifting off the nail bed and he advised bare feet and open shoes. Fine at home, she said, but at school she had to wear shoes. Health and safety. In her mind, however, she could not picture bare legs and feet with a tweed skirt. Apart from anything else, it would be freezing. Yet, saying that, she remembered a young mother, younger than her, ferrying her children to school, her arms completely bare, summer or winter, even in the snow. Alternatively, she could wear shoes two sizes bigger. They talked toes for a moment or two then he typed out a prescription for some rather harsh medication. Later, when she read the folded leaflet enclosed in the box, she doubted that she would be able to complete the course. In recent years, she had noticed when she looked at herself that gradually her lower half had swung away to the left. She could see the twist in her clothes. Physiotherapy or Pilates was suggested to improve her inner strength in an effort to keep her shifting spine aligned. She said that she would check out Pilates classes. And then for the rugby player's itch, which she had intended to get out of the way first because it was so embarrassing. She described how the desire to scratch was intense. Only when it was bleeding and weeping did she stop. Ashamed. She knew what she was doing was wrong, but had no control. It would dry and scab over until the next vicious attack. He scanned down the list of suitable remedies and typed a second prescription. They talked about their children. Hopefully she wouldn't be back for another ten years. And so ended the visit to the health centre.

In an effort to reduce costs and stem the stream of money entering Tesco's bank account every week, she decided to distribute her money more fairly and share it with other high street retailers. Already that week she had shopped in Waitrose and Morrisons, and now it was the turn of the Co-op. She filled two baskets and they were heavy – too heavy: two four-pint bottles of milk, washing powder, tinned tomatoes, pasta and rice and lots of fruit; and of course all the other things. Jill, at the till, was alarmed when she said she was carrying it to the car. Altogether she had five plastic bags, the weight of two alone was too much to carry. They were slippery and awkward. After a few steps, she knew it was too much. Looking back, she should not have even thought that she could do it. The next day her shoulders and arms ached terribly.

She had no plans. After breakfast she just started tidying-up. It seemed to come naturally, which was unusual. Piles of clothes from the loft still lay on the floor where she had started to sort them; washed and ironed holiday clothes sat around waiting to be put away. She sorted drawers and filled a black sack with clothes that she hadn't worn for a while. The denim skirt, she really liked, but it was too straight for her stride and too tight on her bike, and so she didn't wear it. She folded it and placed it along with a Monsoon skirt and top that she also liked, but the skirt was too roomy and she felt old in it. She had seen other women wearing the same fabric, women fatter than her, and that had put her off, so they had been in the drawer for years. And cotton vests that showed up her figure, and a pair of linen trousers that were too loose, and two pairs of flippers and a very good towelling dressing gown that had always been too big for her all went in the sack for Willen Hospice. That left a space in the drawers for the things from the loft. Seeing the progress and the carpet was encouraging. Feeling pleased, she sprayed and polished and dusted the cobwebs and vacuumed the carpets. In the afternoon she went into town and spent a fortune in Boots, buying new DIY implements to sort the toenails, her prescriptions and the recent holiday photos.

There was a choice: it was either yes or no. Having spent the whole week trying to decide which box to tick on the green-coloured memo about school uniform, she was annoyed with herself for returning it late. Apart from her indecision, she wanted to write some comments in the space provided. It required thought. She was afraid of making mistakes, particularly spelling mistakes, putting it aside, avoiding getting on with filling it in, adding to the delay. She spelt "occasionally" wrong. Oh God. She knew what people thought and said when they saw a glaring error. They were cruel. Well, it was better to hand it in with a mistake than not at all, and she wanted to air her views about uniform. She crossed out the s and dropped it in pigeon-hole number one.

The lesson before lunch on Monday morning tested her patience (of which she had plenty) to the limit. She expected an improvement in the pupils' attitude and hoped that they had grown up a little. But no, they came in where they had left off last December, the same. What precisely had they learnt in the past year? Certainly not social skills. For a moment, during the video used to get a flavour of food and ingredients from around the world, she was taken back to her holiday in Brazil. On the video, the chef made a black bean stew with pieces of pork, including pig's ears and even snouts – South American cuisine with African influence. She wanted to say something about the slave trade and her holiday and tell them about the acarajé that she had eaten in Salvador. Did they watch? Were they interested? She paused the video several times to get their attention, without success. The persistent talking was exasperating, the content of which was often inappropriate. A girl reported the boys for talking about "the top half of ladies", then there was a racial comment about chicken masala and one boy managed to fit the stool over himself, like a cage. Apart from four studious girls, most were barking mad, completely out of control. She didn't feel that she had taught them anything, and with that she was disappointed.

She reached into the cupboard under the oven for the pure brilliant white gloss, prised the lid off with a silver dessert spoon, and cut open the confounded vacuum-formed packaging, snugly enclosing the new set of brushes. She and her husband were not in the habit of changing things for the sake of it. She loathed the upheaval and still had not recovered from the gas boiler installation last November. Admittedly, the bathroom had needed attention, but the complete removal of the boxing concealing the pipes hastened the need. She had painted the ceiling weeks ago and her husband had refitted the boxing and replaced the tiles. Lifting the carpet was the next job in order to paint the skirting and the door-frame, but she just couldn't bear the thought of seeing the underlay exposed and the mean rasping gripper round the edges. However, when she walked into the bathroom on Monday evening, the carpet had gone. Wasting no time, she set to, brushing in smooth clean strokes, kneeling and reaching, flexing her wrist. The hard white glossy edge was startling. The smell lingered. Only the wallpapering remained.

The all-singing all-dancing Mamma Mia was a treat – slick and polished, light and entertaining, the classic love story with songs to match. Having tried a couple of times without success, she and her two friends finally got round to seeing it. Four months had slipped past since they had last been to the cinema.

She pulled back the curtains and looked out. The lawn at the front of the house was covered in snow.

Wallpaper paste had improved dramatically in the past twenty years. She remembered it needing two people to mix for a good consistency. It was in the days when she and her husband shared the delights of decorating a room, or rather she was the skivvy stirring the bucket of cold water furiously while he added the sachet of dried paste, complaining if there were lumps because she hadn't stirred quickly enough.

Shit, shit, shit. She realized that, as she was cutting her second length, it was four inches too short. Hanging wallpaper was exacting. She had only bought three rolls; there was no room for mistakes. She planned to start at the window, which she understood to be the correct place. It was a confusing junction: the window-sill, the recess and the partly tiled wall. Incorrect or not, she hung her first pasted length at the door. She would worry about the window in five lengths' time. It was good; everything matched and was trimmed neatly. She stopped at 4.30 p.m., roughly where the shower curtain hung. She re-fitted the roller blind, screwed the shower fitting back to the wall, and cleaned the bathroom, restoring it to its "new" old self.

Wrapping her arms around his legs, she picked up her gangling red setter puppy and sat him awkwardly on her lap. His limbs hung loosely in disarray. She took the palm of her hand from the hard knotty lump between his ears along his smooth sleek back. As she stroked, so his glossy coat disappeared, revealing the fleshy pink skin beneath.

She was walking, carrying her baby son in her arms. As she walked, his eyes changed to milky-white opals, solid and unseeing, his body beneath his skin became soft and hollow, like one of the teddies rescued from the loft.

Her son sat behind, in his seat on the back of her bike. Several times during her bike ride she rode straight off the grassy path into deep dropping spaces, descending into escalators, lifts, mine shafts and crevices, fearlessly oblivious to stairs, machinery, winches and bare rock. It felt a bit clattery but she didn't fall, her bike remained upright, her son intact in his seat.

She hadn't known her brother for long. She came across him, along with other brothers and sisters, while searching for a boy that shared her surname and, until she married, lived at the same address as her. This intrigued her. The extraordinary discovery, quite by chance, of this previous family came to light two years ago when she went to Scotland to find the boy with the same surname as her. Walter, her brother (and, to her, he felt like a brother should feel), was born in the thirties, the youngest of eight children fathered by her father. On Sunday, Walter died and she would no longer be able to see his patient blue eyes, feel his gentleness, hear his quietness, or write "Dear Walter and Jean". For two years he had been the link to her past, the past that until recently she had been oblivious to. She hadn't finished talking to him. There was more to say, more to ask, more to find out. There was never enough time. Although he did have her surname, Walter was not the boy who had shared her address. The boy who had lived with her, she discovered in Australia. He had moved there with his mother in 1949. His name was Donald. His father was her father too. In her father's things she had also come across a photo of a boy and once she had found all her siblings, she naturally assumed the photo to be one of them. It wasn't. Walter's death prompted her to think again about the boy in the small square photograph. It festered at the back of her mind. Who was the boy? She had no names or dates but his photo was important enough to be in her father's belongings and must have meant something to him. Names and places from fifty years ago surfaced in her mind. She longed to know who he was. Enthusiastically, she compiled a list of names and telephone numbers of people she could remember from the fifties.

The prefabs had long gone. He used to live in a prefab with his mum and dad and his brother Derick. His father was disabled and walked with sticks to his blue invalid carriage. His mother was a small scurrying woman. She walked with Tony from the Close where he lived to the Avenue, where she lived, between the fat clipped privet hedges. She took him up the slope to the back door. Her boyfriend was there standing around waiting for her to appear. Her mother hovered and faceless children ran about. Glued to Tony's side, she gave her boyfriend the cold shoulder. He gave her a withering look.

Altogether eighty saucepans boiled and simmered on Monday morning. The smell of pasta bake and spaghetti bolognaise drifted around school.

Her son flew in from New York on his birthday: twenty-three on the 23rd. Before leaving for school she made him a batch of blackberry muffins and left them piled on a plate on the kitchen table, the berries buried in their craters, the juices running and bleeding, turning them purple and filling the house with a heavenly hedgerow smell. Thin splinters of rain painted the window, so unlike the golden Indian summer's day he was born. A birthday dinner was planned for the evening, old favourites were requested, and she had spent the previous evening making a cheesecake and preparing vegetables. The evening stretched into the morning, her youngest son and her eldest son and her. Others had retired to bed or gone home at a sensible hour. Of course, the late night paid her back. Four hours later she sprang out of bed to find her son sprawled over the small settee, in spite of the many cushions, his head resting on her small pile of ironing. As the day progressed she felt steadily worse, feeling weak and fragile. At times she felt faint and starved of air, she longed to lie down.

All too quickly it was time to get her holdall out again. Suddenly it was time to pack for an outdoor weekend at Sedburgh in Cumbria with an all-female party from school. It thrilled her to think that she would be walking again in those triumphant heaving hills. Before that, however, she had to get her lessons ready for Monday. She had to shop and she had to make a spaghetti bolognaise and she had to wash her hair. She had to go to bed, and make bread with year eight on Friday morning and demonstrate how to make a Black Forest gateau to year eleven all within the next twenty-four hours.

Sally, a friend, was going with a young black man. She was buying Sally's house. It had been a good price. It was a big old rambling property in the town. Although she and her husband had bought the house, they went to view it for the first time. The rooms were big and the ceilings high; huge windows overlooked the garden. Sally had young children and they wanted to show them their rooms. They followed the children through the house along a rough stone landing streaming with water. Their feet were wet. Maybe this was why the property cost less than expected. Later they sat round and ate salad at a roughly made table and walked to the river where boats were moored. Sally's first husband, an older man with a spiky modern haircut, came ashore. Excitedly, the children shouted "Daddy, Daddy". Everyone was introduced.

Quite literally she was sandwiched between a rock and a hard place. She tried not to think why she was in a cave at all when there was wall-to-wall blue sky above the limestone pavements. The entrance to the cave was completely obscured by branches and flotsam, swept down by the river and left high and dry as the water receded, woven and tangled like the nest of a giant bird. Clambering over on her stomach, she picked her way through the debris of plastic bottles and rubbish. Only the fact that it had been well washed encouraged her to go forward. Rob, their guide, was a little dismayed and somewhat shocked to see the entrance dammed up, looking like a landfill site in the midst of the surrounding shady beauty. Inside the narrow entrance she was forced to lie flat and crawl commando-fashion to where the cave opened out. She paddled and crawled, her over-suit becoming wet and muddy. Without the beams of their head torches attached to their helmets, it was completely dark. Even with her eyes wide open, it was the blackest, darkest black she had ever seen. Her walk over the Howgill Fells in the afternoon was fantastic. She had no desire to abseil; it was either waiting at the top or waiting at the bottom and she didn't want to wait anywhere, so she walked on her own over the fells with the sheep for company, stopping every few yards on the steepest parts to catch her breath and look at the views, reaching out, sometimes sitting on the soft tufts of grass blown parallel with the land. The activities of the day ended with the aptly named lunatic jump. She had had no intention of getting wet over the weekend but her confidence in the water made her feel reckless. Not one to miss an opportunity, she obediently climbed into a wetsuit and buoyancy aid for the activity. She slithered off the slimy green rocks into the ice-cold water and swam to the other side. Pulling herself up the bank, she waited with the others. She stood on a monstrous rock jutting out over the river. One, two, three. Jump. And she did, surfacing back on the other side. Her legs felt like jelly as she crawled onto the rocks. The friends around encouraged her. She squelched her way back to the minibus thinking about the nice hot shower that would restore and warm her back to reality. The walk the next day to Ingleton Falls was pleasant enough, but didn't compare to the fell-walking the day before.

Heady with fresh air and energized from the walking, she was ready for the dreaded Monday morning. The pupils were tasting and testing four Indian ready-made products. It was simple enough. There were four tables and each was given a product to divide and share and distribute. Each group of pupils was expected to taste and comment, discuss and share their opinions on the sensory qualities of the food. She could not believe how badly some pupils behaved. Their greed was embarrassing and unexpected. She was ashamed of them. Uproar ensued as some of them grabbed and snatched, scooping food from plates that were not theirs. They were incapable of sharing the food fairly and she was glad that she had not given them the responsibility of cooking and serving. It was terrible and she was disappointed; they were fourteen years old. Learning from this behaviour, she decided that for the lesson after break she would divide and serve the food herself. On Friday morning she was demonstrating how to make a Battenburg to year eleven. They gathered round to watch. She sieved the flour.

"That's fine flour, Miss." Which it was, it practically fell through the sieve.

"Yes." She agreed. "It is. But it is self-raising, it is fine self-raising. Ordinary self-raising is fine."

One girl didn't catch the play on words and for her benefit it was repeated. The whole class, including she became sillier and sillier. She hoped that by using marzipan two years past its "best before" date, the pupils would understand that it could still be eaten, it just wouldn't be so good, and that she would not risk them tasting the cake. Knowing them, they would probably have refused anyway. However, she did feed it to her family and they lived to tell the tale (not that she told them the tale of the old marzipan).

October

Nick, her eldest son, was visiting his brother Alex in London. It was the first time he had travelled on his own on the train. She worried. She did not feel confident about his confidence; she wanted to see him off on the platform, to make sure that he didn't end up going the wrong way, and getting stressed, vowing never to go again. She wanted to hold his hand, to show him the way. She was positive and cheery and did not convey her doubt when she dropped him off at the station. He would work it out for himself. Ye of little faith. She collected him on Sunday evening. He had survived not just one night but two, staying up till it was time to get up and breakfasting in the afternoon. Back home, everything seemed tame.

It was a pink gauzy morning, driving her son Guy and his belongings back to London. His bedsit was off the Edgware Road in a quiet, leafy square. Pressing all the right buttons, she parked the car. His room was small. Adequate, but small. It was more a bed-kit than a bedsit. She helped him with his things up several flights of stairs. She suggested moving the bed to behind the door and putting the table near the window. She worried. His clothes would smell of cooking, he would not be able to wander from room to room and there was only the bed or a plastic chair to sit on. She didn't doubt that he would sort it out. She would have liked to be with him longer, to do some shopping or arrange his room, but the thought of getting away from the building traffic of north London bothered her.

She pulled the window closed. Well, not entirely closed. However cold, she had to feel fresh sharp air on her face at night. It had been wide open all summer, but the curtains were blowing into the room and she could hear the rain falling in gusty sheets across the road. Until the heating went on, the chilly prospect of getting up in the morning was daunting. How lucky she had been last weekend to walk bare armed in that wonderful place. And not a moment too soon, yesterday, the first section of the new block paved drive was finished, before the rain set in, washing the blocks and making them shine. As she knew he would be, her husband was pleased with his effort and that of his son, who had worked so hard helping his father, working on his hands and young knees, saving his. Her husband had enjoyed Joe's company.

They came into her room in straggling groups, not listening to instructions and not ready to learn. Eventually they were seated how she wanted them to be. Determined to have her say, she had arranged the stools in a loose circle. She had opened each booklet and laid the low-level work on the table so that they could see how bad it was. She started quietly, explaining how disappointed she was at their behaviour last Monday. She said that that particular lesson had been enjoyed by pupils for many years and that she had never ever seen such appalling behaviour. She asked them to look at the work on the table. It was dreadful. From most, it was slapdash, even written in crayon. Then she launched into talking about their options that they would decide on in the New Year. She said that all the work on the table was ungraded and she would not want them in her group. In full flight she continued, saying that she expected the lesson to be excellent and that she would phone any offending pupils' parents at 3.30 p.m. if it wasn't. With that they all got on.

Although she couldn't feel it, her feet were caked in mud. She washed it off in the bath. Overnight, the earth had crept up the bath and onto the newly hung wallpaper. Resembling an ant's nest, a thin crust had formed on the surface of the fine loose earth, crumbling when she touched it with her finger. The dampness had eaten into the wallpaper, lifting it from the wall, frayed and disintegrating like thin wet newspaper.

She plucked up courage to make some phone calls from the list of names drawn up a few weeks ago. Never expecting to be so lucky, the very first person she called was the wife of her father's drinking partner. She thought as she dialled that it might be one of their many sons, still living in the area. After introducing herself, a visit was arranged.

The lady from the handbag shop appeared from the Arcade. Smiling, they exchanged hellos on passing and immediately she felt a pang of guilt because she had not been back to buy another handbag. After being talked into buying a soft, brown, leather bag, she remembered saying not to rely on her as a regular customer as she had no need for more than one bag at a time and, lovely though they were, she saw no point in accumulating bags for the sake of it.

She was in the kitchen at the back of the house, kneeling on the work surface, cleaning the window and she hadn't heard the postman. There, on the mat, was a card saying that there was a parcel awaiting collection at the local office and even though it gave her son's initial, she knew that it would be the book. She called in to collect it before swimming. It was too early. She went back. It was not the book. The A2 size envelope was for her other son, not even for the one named on the card. It was the second parcel in recent weeks. The previous one her neighbour had accepted from the postman and, seeing her pull up in the car, she went indoors to get it. Instantly her thoughts flew to her book. It would be the book. She was so excited when her neighbour returned with a box. Her hopes were totally destroyed when she saw that it was a box of longlife light bulbs, distributed free, courtesy of British Gas.

She had a list of jobs as long as her arm for the weekend. At the top of the list was the word "wallpaper". She had kept the leftover paste from the bathroom to fix the paper in the kitchen that had come adrift. Years ago, when she transformed the kitchen, she had not removed the radiator and subsequently the paper behind it had dried and peeled off where tea towels and wet socks had been hung in the winter. The paper was hard and brittle and easily torn; in fact, there was a tear. She started by soaking the paper with a wrung out cloth, to make it malleable. Carefully she prised it from behind the radiator and coated the reverse side with wallpaper paste, leaving it to soak in, returning later to press it down again, reaching with the palm of her hand flat and hard in the narrow gap between the wall and the radiator. What she should do was to do a course in plumbing. Also on the list was the word "potato". There because the two sacks bought by her husband a week ago were emitting the most foul smell that seeped into the house via the airing cupboard. At first she thought that the smell was coming from the left-out-in-the-rain tent, but it was too disgusting for that. She sifted through both sacks, decanting the potatoes into clean ones, the offending potatoes removed. Her friend, Chris, was on the list. She phoned before swimming to say that she would be with her around three o'clock. They caught up with their news. A flare up in her rheumatoid arthritis had rendered her friend unable to do her garden, her passion. They talked about suicide and the banking crisis and Brazil, even unfolding a map of the Amazon basin. Her friend's mother had recently died. Wasn't it enough to be a daughter and next-of-kin? Why was it assumed that there had to be anything else? Even though bound by blood, why did people think that you had to be fond of the dead person lying there? Why did people assume when they didn't know you from Adam? Her friend had not been loved, not really loved. She knew how she felt. Not all children loved their parents. Blood is not always thicker than water.

Her son was wearing what was known as his flying suit, a blue all-in-one, zip-fronted, padded nylon suit worn to keep out the cold. He wore his red Wellington boots. The whole family were coming down the mountain, past long gardens, dark with compacted earth, laid out ready to be turfed, quickening their pace as they neared the bottom. They crossed into a stream and all managed easily, except her small son; the water came up to his chest, filling his boots and his suit. She grasped his hand pulling him towards the bank.

The robin was there, hopping about, waiting for her to unearth something interesting to eat. He would listen, his head on one side as she chatted to him. She liked to think that he understood what she was saying. His cheeky confidence brought him closer and closer, close enough for her to touch. But she knew he would have fluttered away had she tried. She scrabbled around on her hands and knees, pulling weeds and forking over the ground, leaving it ready for the winter weather to do its work. For mid-October it was blissfully warm, the air was soft and the sun shone, shadows, deep and long, stretched across the garden. Maybe for the last time this year she placed her deckchair on a puddle of sunny grass under the clear blue sky. She read until she fell asleep. The weekly trip to the cinema had gone by the by, but on Monday after school she and her two friends went to see The Boy in the Striped Pyjamas. The end was so final and the three of them came out, for once, lost for words.

She glided into Euston on a thankfully late Virgin train, non-stop. Waiting on the platform. Had she got time for a coffee? She peered along the track. No, she could see a pair of lights in the distance and decided, having unexpectedly caught the fast train, not to risk losing it. As it happened, she sat next to the buffet car. Slowly she sipped her fair trade latte. It doubled up as lunch, for certainly there would not be time for that. Her quest to find the hat, seen in the *Telegraph* several weeks ago, led her (after the meeting in a Holborn hotel) to Knightsbridge. She checked Harvey Nichols and Harrods. Neither had a hat department. She took herself to Fenwicks and Selfridges, where each had a small selection. The nearest thing to her feathery Frankie Morello hat that she so desired was something called a fascinator. It sounded like something from the Edwardian underworld, something disturbing and shockingly scandalous. Indeed, as the word suggests, they were fascinating and they were feathery. She would have to rethink the hat; she had spent enough time on it. At six thirty she met Alex and Guy for a meal at the usual place in Charlotte Street. She hurried in the lurking dark to her car. She did not feel completely safe.

How could her husband make so much noise simply breathing? She lay very still trying to go to sleep, her legs tired and threatening cramp. Exasperated, she shushed him and momentarily he stopped in the still, warm night, only to resume seconds later. It was no good. Taking her pillow, she slipped silently out of bed and crept under the duvet in her son's empty room.

She tried on her blue velvet dress. It was over twenty years old and always kept for best. The thick blue was still lovely but she planned a daring change with an insert of tartan silk. It was a difficult dress to put on and even worse to take off. The sleeves were straight and tight, designed to be so, and the fabric had no give whatsoever. Once on, it moulded snugly. When removing the dress inside out she sometimes heard a stitch break and she would try to stay calm. Still inside out she laid the dress flat on the bed, matching the side seams, and took her shears, still with traces of wallpaper paste on, and cut through the pile along the dusty French chalk line. Small clouds puffed up against the midnight blue as she cut. Guided by the check of the tartan she measured a band of silk and joined it at the ends to form a circle. This, she attached to the velvet she had cut off and deftly her fingers eased the two together. This was then attached to the skirt of the dress. She made a matching ribbon for the waist.

The cake was too inviting. It was covered in delicate yellow icing and it sat in its own paper case on the table, lighting up the surrounding chaos of the storeroom. She was in the storeroom at half past three when four boys burst in. Two were collecting folders. The temptation was too great. They all looked at the cake.

"Don't touch the cake." She took her eyes off it for a second. The cake had gone. All four denied all knowledge and the inevitable paper trail followed. The two boys collecting folders assured her that it wasn't them. Well, that left the other two.

The occasion for the new dress was Guy's graduation, celebrated fittingly at the Royal Albert Hall. Its round red warmth matched the pleasure in her heart. A table had been booked for 12.30 p.m. at a restaurant in Gloucester Road. Her son was not truly convinced that the day would go to plan and emailed an itinerary the evening before. Nerves.

Hello,

Here is my plan for tomorrow.

09:00 Order my photos

10: 00 Go to the first hour of my lecture

11:15 Collect my gown and have my photo taken (11:30 is the earliest that I am allowed to collect my gown). Take my gown off and leave it in my office.

12:30 Meet you outside Med Kitchen

14:00 Go to college (on the way to Royal Albert Hall). Look round my lab, pick my gown back up and you can take some pictures of me.

15:00 Go to Royal Albert Hall (just across the road). Be seated by 15:15.

18:00 Champagne and canapés across the road in college.

Love Guy x

Well, it went exactly to plan as she knew it would. It was a very special day.

Anxious to go before the dark evenings drew in, she phoned and asked if she could call on Saturday afternoon. Iris opened the door. There was instant recognition, even though they had not seen each other for fifty years. Iris stooped and shuffled in her slippers, but she was keen, keen as mustard, searching her memory, sparking and firing, remembering people and places. She took a reunion picture from the display cabinet and named the people in it. Between them, they remembered where they lived and what they did, piecing the forgotten jigsaw back together again. They talked about Guides and she told Iris that every time she made a bed, even though she had fitted sheets, she thought about envelope corners and doing her bed-maker's badge at nine o'clock one Saturday morning at Brown Owl's house. Iris's husband was in many of the family pictures. He was how she remembered him. Lean. Iris had grown up in the same village as her and had met her husband when he was building the prefabs after the war, the very prefabs that she had recently dreamed about. She passed her the picture of the boy. She had no idea who he was but she did say something that was possibly a clue. She said that her father was living with another woman before his wife arrived from Scotland. She was only surmising, but was the boy in the photograph their son?

The awful feeling of doom and gloom because of the clocks going back and summer time officially ending was put on hold temporarily while her husband fished on the rocky shore of Lake Chira. Even in September he would start. "The clocks go back next month." Then, nearer the time, he would say, "The clocks go back next week." Then, before going to bed he would go round the house changing the time on all the clocks. It must be an old people's thing, like reading the obituaries in the local paper.

The autumn break was unexpected. Years ago she said that she would never go on another fishing holiday, but the photos on the website looked good and the solitude appealed. She could read and write and do her marking. The previous Friday she and her friend had sat on high stools having a coffee, talking about the forthcoming holiday. She said that her expectations were not high. Her friend was looking forward to her holiday in the Lake District. But she replied saying that she didn't especially like the idea of driving and stopping and looking at the scenery, faces etched with a mixture of concern and boredom. It was something that old people did and her parents had done. She admitted that the fishing holiday was not her cup of tea either.

Adjusting overnight was hard and on her first day she had achieved very little. At the airport, she bought a Sunday newspaper, expecting it to last all week. She read about the state of the economy and the US elections and the supplement on sex.

It was based on statistical evidence and apart from the interviews with the nurse, the saleswoman and the censor, it was staid and dull. She herself remembered how it used to be. She remembered Pan's People on Top of the Pops and Ready Steady Go on Saturday evenings, her mother squirming uncomfortably, shocked and embarrassed at pop stars gyrating. She would have turned away and drawn air through clenched teeth to see two men kissing, and got up and left the room at full-on-sex. It wasn't new.

Once established, they settled into a routine: her husband fishing, away for nearly twelve hours, and for her, a nice long stretch of time to do nothing more than nothing, just walking or sitting on the terrace overlooking the village, soaking up the sun, reading and thinking and dreaming. Bliss. Apart from the cockerel cock-a-doodle-doing, nothing was doing. Nothing much stirred in the afternoons. The great weight of air hung heavy and still. For whole empty days she didn't do a thing. It was a lovely spot, scattered white houses, some with flat roofs and some with gently sloping warm terracotta tiles. Flies buzzed and settled on bare skin. They nipped, not quite allowing total peace. Occasionally, she heard tyres on the rough gravel road, twisting up and away from the village. Birds twittered, and in the distance dogs chorused, howling and lamenting in unison. Around her a soft, feathery wind blew. It was hard work doing nothing. On and off she read. It was a luxury not usually afforded. Only in the holidays could she devote time to reading books. Sometimes the air was scented. She had smelt it before; it smelled of Spain.

The dark, inky shadows below her eyes disappeared and she felt untroubled. What she did love was to see her husband, pleased and smiling, catching fish. She often felt with the rush of work that she didn't see anything, but being isolated and alone heightened her senses; his accuracy in placing the bait, insisting on the right spot to attract the fish, his patience and endeavour in waiting, his confidence, his strength in playing the fish and his care and respect for the gentle creature lying in his arms.

Clouds rushed across the ocean of sky; the blue space left behind hurriedly filled with more. She went in and out, testing the temperature. Now and then there was a great shushing in the pines, then calm; a dense thick heavy calm. Brooding clouds erupted and fell, spilling a veil of rain, so light that it felt like pin pricks on her hot skin. Slinking feral cats kept close to walls. The cloud persisted and later fell as drizzle and then as rain, straight down and steely grey. The next day blades of neon sparked out of the ground, ignited.

She was more than thankful to have packed her walking boots, as she walked several times a day to sit for a while with her husband. The path to the rocky shore of the lake was loose and rough. Although not afraid of heights, she did not look down. A stew of rocks merged and swam about. Danger was imminent. The abrupt precipice just fell away, right beside the sole of her boot. She did not take her eyes off the narrow haphazard path that climbed around the side of the mountain, interrupted with outbreaks of rocks and boulders – if not careful, there to trip her up. Picking out the path was difficult; really, there was no path, and until she was used to the terrain she was anxious, like seeing the pool full of splashing bodies and wondering how she would swim twenty lengths or negotiating the traffic through north London when she couldn't see the road for traffic, or finding herself standing in front of a child, thinking: what is his name? Then, just at the crucial moment, his name would pop out of her mouth as though she had known it all along. Here and there she could see the tread of her boots and her husband's trainers, already smudging and softening. Soaring buzzards called and spiralled.

The mountain sat like a great armchair presiding over the stillness, its arms threadbare from the leaching, hurrying cloud and the bleaching white light of the sun. Over millions of years the wind had slowly worn and weathered. Her walk to the dam took her through the village. Unusually, some doors were open, and from the inner darkness she could hear the swish of a broom on cool, tiled floors. As she walked, she thought of Spain, of cigarettes, of graffiti, of closed doors and plastic bags, supermercados Quevedo Ramirez and Siempre Precios Bajos mercadona and Spar, all casually thrown, casually dumped, left by the side of the road. She spent time on the rocky beach with her husband, sitting quietly on a rock-hard rock, her bum numb. A fragile, white lacy web of roots clinging to the rocks and fibrous plants, knotted into the fabric of the earth, lay exposed, like tousled orange string, sprawling and splayed out over the rocks, waiting to be buoyant again, free to float and drift in the current when the winter rains returned and filled the lake. The wind that leapt around the valley decided how the lake would wear her dress. Sometimes, when there was none, it was glassy calm, chocolatey smooth, woven in satin. Sudden flurries would ripple the surface into frilly ruffles, golden sunlight, a shimmering mesh, strengthening winds swirled and ruched, stressed and crumpled, bows and darts kicking out, streaming corrugated pleats deep in mountain shadow. Dimples and splashes of beads danced across the fabric. A rainbow ribbon streamed in a rushing cloudy sky.

By Thursday, they were quite literally on the breadline as there were only two slices of bread left to eat. Then, by chance, Heinz knocked and called.

"Hola, Hola."

He brought an umbrella and a harvest of tomatoes, a red pepper, an authentic Spanish onion and two warm loaves. "Muchas gracias."

"Con mucho gusto." Pleased, he turned away. "Adios." With the provisions, she made a thick tasty pulp and called it soup. She served it in a bowl and ate it with a fork, using the bread to mop up the liquid. It wasn't the first time that Heinz had brought food. He had brought bread and the ultimate comfort food, a fruit loaf, freshly baked. With her husband's dislike for dried fruit she knew that she would be eating it all, on its own, with tea, with coffee, with wine. In a way it spoiled her lean living and she did not want her efforts to stay fit abandoned. What she didn't like was the heavy sludgy feeling from overeating way beyond what usually sustained, with no way of using up its energy. Not eating fruit when she was away was a failing of hers and with that in mind the emailed shopping list was fairly fruity. They had been warned that there were no supermercados in Chira. There really was no chance of overeating.

They had just walked from Bar Vista Alegae when, amazingly, and as promised, Matthew proudly delivered to their kitchen table, a pizza freshly made by his wife, the tray still hot through the oven mitts. They had met Matthew on their first night and he spoke fluent English. He took them to a bar, nothing short of an Aladdin's cave. The walls and ceiling were bursting with hardware: paella pans, brooms, buckets and hurricane lamps. Under the counter, and camouflaged in the walls, was the alcohol. Cold beers were fetched from the fridge in the corner by the door and she had a vino tinto, taking the open bottle with her when she left.

Her eyes filled with tears as she neared the end of The Book Thief. The holiday too was ending and the nights were drawing in and her husband would be complaining and it would be cold and wet in England and she hadn't done the marking. She reached for a tissue and dabbed her eyes.

All week the marking had lain on the table, wrapped in a carrier bag, gnawing at her conscience, making her feel guilty. It finally got the better of her at the airport. Surely, in two hours, she could make a start. Now and then she lifted her head and looked around. Opposite, was a woman, also with a red biro in her hand, flicking ticks and crosses across the pile of pages on her lap.

Looking down on the airport as they escaped from Madrid was like looking at the Lego models her children used to construct across their bedroom floor. Their eyes keen, scanning the brightly coloured pieces in the base of an old suitcase. She could hear them above her when she was in the kitchen, scratching and burrowing, looking for a twoer or a helmet, concentrating, determined to find whatever it was. She too was good at looking and finding the vital piece and would join in, kneeling with them beside the case, scratching and searching. They would be pleased when she found the missing piece. Making a model could take days. "Take a picture Mummy." And she would and now, when she came across the finished Lego worlds amongst the photos, she smiles to herself. Such a long time ago. Like a good mummy, she would take them a warm drink and something freshly baked from the oven on a tray. On a warm sunny day everything would transfer to the garden. They would sit on their haunches or cross-legged or stretched out on their fronts, elevated on elbows. They would organize themselves. One would make all the people, one would make all the vehicles, one would make all the buildings and one would be at school, then two would be at school, then three would be at school and one would make everything. The case was now in the loft waiting for the inevitable.

November

With earnest the marking started on Monday evening, sitting side-saddle on the settee, the world atlas on her knee, writing furiously. She loathed and despised the intrusion of the marking in "her" time, in "her" sitting room. Even seeing the names of some pupils wrung her out. Not only did she have to put up with them in the classroom, but on holiday and at home. God damn it! Italy is shaped like a boot. Don't they know anything? Italy was plunged into the Barent Sea to freeze to death and the Galapagos Islands were renamed Britain. In red pen she wrote "sp" by spelling mistakes, of which there were many. There was "nuffing" for "nothing", "oneones" for "onions", "glofes" for "gloves", "uvon gruvs" for "oven gloves", and "toawl" for "towel". Vegetables had been the key ingredients and had several connotations; the pupils seemed to have great difficulty spelling it. Randomly, she jotted down the variations: "vegtibals", "vegdebules", "vegtabels", "vegables", "vegertables", "vegetabales", "vegdables", "vegtebels". It might be better to reduce the word to "veg" and be finished with it; they might manage to spell that. There were many more mistakes, but she had seen them before.

Since early September, she had kept her eye on a particular lace dress. She felt that she would look nice in it, different and neat, not mutton dressed as lamb and not frumpy either. It was dangerously black, but the brown sequins caught the light and the subtle brown lacy inserts distracted. She withstood the longing to go home and, instead, stopped at the shops to look at it again. She pressed her pound into the meter and pressed the green button. She gave herself an hour. In the shop she even went as far as removing the dress from the rail. She held it to her and placed it over her arm, along with an irresistible black taffeta skirt and a little black dress. Step two. "Cubicle number seven, on the right." She locked the door and removed her clothes. After trying on each thing twice she was still undecided. She liked all three and in the end asked the assistant to keep them all till the following day when she would return with her friend. Retracing her steps the next day, she tried them on again, starting with the skirt. Her friend leaned patiently at the entrance to the fitting rooms while she flounced in and out. Yes, it looked good, but it was black. Then she tried the little black dress; it felt so comfortable and it made her feel young, but it was black. Then she tried the black/brown lace dress. Immediately she could tell by her friend's face that it was the one. She asked her friend to fetch a muff from the next department. It went perfectly. Now all she needed was a hat and something to cover her bare shoulders.

They hadn't been in her classroom for two minutes when a mixing bowl was sent crashing to the floor. Luckily it was metal but none the less she sent them all outside the room again to calm down. She spoke severely, raising her voice as she had done last week and for a moment they were quieter.

Of course, she tried to ignore the run-up to Christmas, but despite that, the pressure was on. Already, in her mind, she was planning meals and writing a mental shopping list. The shops and the media had got it covered. She tended to avoid being swept along until the last possible minute, usually when she was driving out of the car park on the last day of term. Tesco was crammed with displays of festive spirits and "must-haves" that for a whole year had been managed without. As she left the shop on Tuesday morning with a trolley-load-of "wul", a tacky display of a double bed caught her attention. It was like a bed in a brothel, or how she imagined one to be. It was covered in a lurid maroon satin brocade duvet and matching pillows. On the tables each side of the bed were annoying little Christmas decorations, cheap and gaudy. How could anyone think that it looked good? On the other hand, Marks & Spencer were promoting Christmas with a "Delicious Drama" – an epic lasting two minutes, set in a grand country house, insincere people handing out lavish presents, beautifully made-up, smart suits and glamorous dresses, affluent luxury and affluent smiles, ringing with false laughter. Christmas is coming and she wasn't in the mood. So desperate were the shops to shift stock that a frenzy of sales commenced, 20% off here, half-price there, reductions and tempting offers too good to miss. She ignored them.

She made a habit of checking her publisher's website just to see if there was any progress with her book. Something was wrong. She was unable to access it; the blue bar along the bottom barely moved. It remained frozen until the next day, but in that time her confidence lurched. Her son had also checked and phoned her later with bad news. Spam, as far as she was concerned, was something to eat. It was pink and came in a round tin. When she was at school it was sliced, coated in batter and deep-fried. The writers on the blog were scathing and rasping with nothing good to say. All her hopes and dreams were shattered. In the past eight months she had become complacent. After all the excitement and anticipation she felt let down, dropped from a great height, deflated and defeated. How could anyone flatter her into thinking that what she had to say was worth publishing? Did they send out a standard evaluation report on all the manuscripts? How could it all end in such an anticlimax? She had been so trusting, so innocently gullible, naïve. She understood now why she hadn't seen their name engraved in the granite at Bermuda Square and why the cashier at the post office queried the post code. She couldn't believe that she could be so deceived, so taken in, so tempted. She felt demoralized and disappointed. Duped and dumped, that's how it felt. She didn't share her concerns with her husband. She didn't want to trouble him or to give him the opportunity to be pessimistic and dampen her spirits still further. In life there were far worse things that could happen. Her book was still there on the list of upcoming titles, but the whole episode left a sour note. The underlying nervous excitement faded, to be replaced with an underlying fear of failure. She always knew that it would be a gamble.

Where there were trees, their boots kicked through the bones of leaves, lying curling and crisp, waiting for rain to anchor them down, returning them to the soil. The day was bright and sunny and very cold. She had taken advantage of her son being home, and in the afternoon wrapped up and went out for a walk. The circular walk was slightly more rural than their usual man-made walk. It took them across fields, over stiles and through farmyards. They saw black-faced sheep and cows standing braced against the brisk north wind. Where tractors had churned up the tracks they had to negotiate puddles and saturated ground, their boots becoming heavy with mud. Winter wheat had been sown and blades of green bravely endured in the bare windswept fields. The forecast of a cold weekend was fairly accurate and, although they had escaped the worst, as they usually did, she woke to a raw, wet day and spent it trying to master PowerPoint presentations, making dinner and dealing with her son's laundry, which, apart from what he was wearing, seemed to be the entire contents of his wardrobe.

The thought of her Monday morning groups was daunting. She had planned good lessons and failed to see why the pupils should be so obnoxious. One pupil was absent and one was in inclusion, both instigators of noise and general mayhem. A girl in the group after break was mute, doing her bit for charity week. She demonstrated decorating six small cakes to the class. The boy on her left said that the piping bag looked like a big condom. "Well, you'd certainly be boasting if you had one as big as that," she said as she piped butter-cream rosettes around the cup cake. Confused embarrassment spread across his face. Laughter broke out amongst those who were listening. Those who weren't, wanted to know what she had said, suddenly interested. By lunchtime it had all passed. That's what her husband says. "It will all pass." And it does.

On Tuesday she caught sight of a boy in her class who picked up his rolling-pin and, turning it on its end, slipped it up and down through his loosely closed hand. She reminded him that the rolling-pin was for rolling dough. And then on Wednesday, as soon as she had said, "Then pour half a pint of milk in your jugs," she was once again in for some laughter from the boys. They tittered in schoolboy fashion, drawing curvy bodies in the air. She had heard jug jokes before when she called for the girls in the end kitchen to put their jugs away. It was harmless fun.

A lot of words beginning with v spilled onto the page, capturing her anger, her hurt and her disappointment. Vanity, virtual, vexed, vain, valid, valuable, varnish, veneer, vent, venture, vermin, verve, violate, vanish, voice, vulnerable, vulgarity, voyage. Strong words. She could hear people, "I thought you were getting a book published." And her trying to justify and explain what had happened and why it hadn't happened. She was down to earth, feet planted firmly; not the sort to have the wool pulled over her eyes, someone who called a spade a spade, open and sincere. Throwing caution to the wind, she sealed the envelope containing the final "up-front" instalment for the publication of her book.

She could see by its absence that it had gone. In the past two years the sycamore had changed from a child to an adolescent, growing uncontrollably, reaching up and stretching out, outgrowing its space in the corner of the front garden. It had gone to make way for the final section of the new drive. The weight of leaves would no longer spiral golden to the ground then scamper and eddy round and round to drift by the wall at the front door, and she would miss their gentle pattering in the spring but not the ghostly sound of the wind in its boughs, twisting and writhing. The trunk lay like a caber beside the fence, and the branches were stacked, ready to be cut into logs for the winter fires, on the chimenea.

On Friday morning she dared herself to give a PowerPoint presentation. She was perfectly honest with the pupils and said that the technology was new to her and to forgive her if it all went wrong. They were much more knowledgeable than her and were pleased to offer advice when needed. They would be able to see that she was not very confident, slow using the mouse and cautious using the keyboard. However, she did her slide show on technical terms and they made notes in their books. She had to start somewhere.

Instead of having a Christmas tree, or as well as, she thought she might use some of the sycamore's finer branches to create a display, painting them with white emulsion, binding them together and putting them in one of her stone pots, kept especially for such arrangements. She left a note for her husband on the kitchen table to cut her a bundle of twigs three feet long. In her heart she knew that having no tree would be the thin edge of the wedge. She herself could not entertain the idea of a synthetic tree, its branches folded up and stored in a box. It simply could not compete with the real thing. A real tree had a loving glow and a lingering pineforest smell. A real tree was full of magic and expectation. She would not be able to bear the disappointment on her children's faces and in their voices, if she didn't have a real tree. They had always had a real tree.

The Good Food Show had finally rolled round. She and her two friends had bought tickets weeks ago and because of maintenance work on the railway line, took, instead, the coach to Birmingham. It dropped them off at the airport where they hopped on the monorail for the NEC. In the capsule they shared chatty banter with Tim and Rob, bike enthusiasts, going to the Bike Show, also at the NEC. They said that if they went to the Isle of Man trade stall to mention their names. Mentioning their names paid off: they were treated to dressed crab and the most divine scallops and other tasty morsels. They tasted their way up and down the aisles of exhibitors, snippets of chocolate and slivers of cheese and thimblefuls of wines and spirits. The highlight was lunch, which lasted hours and could have gone on; not that the food was particularly amazing but they could sit and talk over a couple of bottles of wine, watching the world go by. Retracing their steps, they went back to buy cheese, pies, crisps, pickles and scallops. Blank faces watched and listened to demonstrations. Whether it was the latest steamer or the ultimate floor mop, people stood around like sheep, staring, not in the least interested, just stopping because others had, afraid to miss out on some bargain. Greedy people pushed in and pushed past to get at stalls offering free samples; staff barely had time to replenish the plates before they were emptied.

Like last Sunday, it was cold and wet. She went with her husband to visit his mother. They found her in bed asleep. Under the duvet, her waterlogged legs lay thick and heavy. How old she looked, a shrinking shadow, her face still with a yellow tinge and her eyes hollow. "Hello mum." Yet, when she surfaced and knew who they were, her jumbled thoughts spilled from her mouth. In a loop she repeated things over and over again. She asked her son why he had painted his hair white, forgetting that he too had aged. Senility, the burden of old age. By the time they reached the door she had forgotten they had been.

December

All week the cold, glass mornings penetrated, temperatures barely above freezing. Even in the afternoon the windscreen was iced over, the winter sky clear and frosty. The more comfortable brown shoes were determining the colour scheme, and on Thursday she wore her brown angora jumper with a feather trim. Excitement broke out when the two boys saw the jumper: unable to resist they innocently touched and stroked its softness, oblivious to the protocol. "Miss has got that jumper on again." Forgetting how they would react, she shook them off. She must remember not to wear the jumper on Thursdays and Fridays.

She held the four babies close. Each was wrapped tightly, cocooned in a printed flannelette sheet, their lolling heads supported. Only one baby was hers. It had a downy head of hair and a smooth peach-soft face. In the half-light, collapsing buildings reared up out of the street, left hanging and gaping, their innards gouged out. She trampled along with the babies through the crumbling devastation, numb. Her own baby troubled her and on waking from the dream realized that the baby in her arms was herself.

She had the treasured day to herself and spent it doing some much-needed autumn cleaning. She was hoovering the cobwebs that were lacing themselves around the coving in the kitchen when the brush attachment dislodged a piece of paper, which until that moment was completely hidden on top of a cupboard above the oven. She pulled up a chair and reached for it. It was thick with grease and very discoloured, but still legible. It was a note, written by her son in 2001 then updated in 2008. Still standing on the chair, she read it: "In 10 years time I promise to paint the skirting board in my room magnolia if mum wants me to. (If I'm not here.) May 2001. Painted white, July 2008." On the back and even fainter there was another note. "Dad says I will still be living here in 2011." Dated May 2001.

Glancing out of the bedroom window as she was getting ready to go out in the brittle cold afternoon, she saw on the road the remains of a McDonalds, discarded, left to be crushed flat and bleed to orange. Even from upstairs she could see the brown paper bag torn open, the plastic ketchup, the cardboard burger box and the drinks holder all scattered across the road along with a handful of chips. She was not "lovin' it". Rubbish randomly thrown was one of her pet hates, and with that she tore off a black bin liner and went outside to retrieve the litter, leaving the chips for the audience of gulls that had been watching the proceedings from the ridge tiles opposite. They swooped down to eat before she reached the front door.

Her friend was complaining about her daughter being partial to particular carrier bags. She hardly dared to admit to her friend that she too was a bag lady. Not that she kept her belonging in bags; on the contrary, she was a collector of bags and understood where her daughter was coming from. How could she explain her fetish for carrier bags? She didn't go out of her way to acquire a different bag; it was more like memorabilia, a reminder of what she had bought and where she had bought it so she could remember. Long before the word "recycling" had been invented she had kept bags, folding them carefully in half and then in quarters, pressing the air out with the palm of her hand. Even now she had a drawer full, some going back years. She didn't use them for shopping, she didn't use them for anything. God knows what she was keeping them for? Occasionally an interesting bag would find its way into the bin, discarded by a pupil. They didn't know what they were missing. It was like tin foil: she was never generous with foil, it was expensive. The pupils expected it, almost demanding it, to cover their food products. She didn't remember her mother using foil, but remembered instead her using butter wrappers, and they were used over and over again. They didn't realize how fortunate they were.

She had finally given up on finding the hat of her dreams and decided instead to make one. Carefully, she unpicked the ostrich feather from around the neck of the much-loved-by-everyone brown angora jumper and attached it with pins to a brown felt hat, its brim removed. The look was exactly what she wanted. Deep in her pillow, she could hear her heart beating. Unable to sleep with the excitement, on Wednesday morning she got up early and sat immediately under the 60w bulb in the dining room, painstakingly stitching the feather trim to the felt through the grosgrain ribbon with big strong stitches.

Although the invitation had only recently been received, she had known about her niece's wedding for nearly a year, thus the need for the lacy dress and the feathery fun. The only drawback was that it was to be on the first day of the Christmas holiday, which, as far as she was concerned, was the worst possible day of the entire year. By then she would be completely knackered, her eyes a halo of blue, and her skin tired and beige. All she wanted to do was to go for a walk, to step off the treadmill, wind down and chill out before her children descended for the festive onslaught. But no, with the urgency of a wildebeest she stampeded on.

She took to writing lists, crossing off things done and things bought, revising and re-writing fresh lists on sheets of folded A4 paper. How could the wedding be only a week away? Gusting winds dragged the crows around the sky. The rain fell in sheets. Over the weekend she chose cards and bought stamps, wrote them, briefly remembering each recipient, and posted them in one heavy descending bundle. She crossed it off the "to-do" list. Not on the list, was "buy-a-dishwasher". How could her loyal friend and ally let her down at this crucial time of year? She spent the weekend washing up by hand. There was even a bonding moment when her husband picked up the tea towel and moved it around the plates. She was not alone.

She had a week to mark the most recent projects. To mark the occasion, and the projects, she bought two red biros. Each evening she perched on the edge of the settee, stopping when sleep insisted, and continuing again at five the next morning. "I fort the pinapel was dilishes". By Tuesday evening the new dishwasher had been installed, courtesy of her friend making a phone call and the local shop delivering it pronto, and by Thursday evening, she had broken the back of the marking. There was "nuffing" that was worthy of being displayed on the wall.

She was greeted at the church by her sister. She should see her sister more often. For twenty years she had hidden herself away deep in the country, devoting her time to renovating. It hadn't done her any good. In that time she had systematically and deliberately lost her outstanding beauty. She stood in the entrance to the church: gaunt, her skin creeping around her swan-like neck, like an undernourished elderly relation. She was only fifty-five. Maybe that was the look she desired and hankered after. Clever, she was undoubtedly clever. Other people might be swept along with her grand designs and high ideals but she didn't pull the wool over her eyes. Her sister introduced her to her friends, like her, health professionals from work, and in that brief encounter she could tell who ruled the waves, imposing her thoughts and opinions, because they couldn't think for themselves. Could they not see beyond the façade?

She was glad that she hadn't bought a fascinator. She stood at the back of the church and could see other women in the congregation were wearing them. They had an economy about them and she was so glad to be in a real hat. Her vantage point was not good, standing behind all the tall, suited men on the groom's side; and it all happened at such a pace. She wanted to rewind and play it again at 33 r.p.m. She wanted to admire her beautiful niece as she walked with her father down the aisle to her waiting husband to be. She wanted to see her radiant glow, to capture her vitality, she wanted to catch her eye and smile, she wanted to reach out and touch her dress and work out how the technicalities of the train pulled up like a Venetian blind. But within a second she had gone. The ushers should have ushered her to the front where she could have pondered the proceedings instead of listening to the boring vicar, too full of his own self-importance. Having a captive audience, he used the opportunity as a recruitment drive to swell conversion, implying that the people before him needed to change their ways. Bravely and confidently her sister recited "The Song of Wondering Aengus" by W. B. Yeats. She was fluent and articulate, every comma and full stop accentuated, words perfectly formed. There was texture and clarity in her expression. As clear as night air, her sister's voice resonated around the country church in the silence of the winter afternoon. Warmed with mulled wine, the congregation mingled until it was time to be seated for the reception in The Tithe Barn. It was a bit like the party Mr Boldwood gave his labourers in *Far from the Madding Crowd*. Once the toasts and the speeches had been made the tables were cleared to make room for the dancing. That was the best bit and over too soon. She danced all around the barn with anyone and everyone. Where were the songs that her children had chosen? She reckoned that the D.J. had chosen the songs. They had his signature, and it was just fluky if it happened to be one they had chosen. Her niece had requested "no cheese please"; there was plenty of cheese. Just after twelve she and her husband said their goodbyes. The tense, arm-hugging cold brought them close. Linking arms, they huddled together, his hands stuffed in his pockets and hers in her muff. They walked back along the dark, high-banked lanes to the rambling old house where they were staying. Apart from her clattering stilettos assuring her that she was on the road and not wandering across some field, there was no other sound, not a lumbering badger or a "lane-wise" owl. Gradually, their eyes adjusted and became accustomed to the darkness. Quietly, they opened and closed the great oak door, padded through the house and up the wide carpeted stairs to their room. Water unfurled like silk from the tap. As usual, she woke too early and lay feeling frail, falling in and out of sleep until the grey mists of morning rolled into the room. As she knew she would, she had to decline the most wonderful breakfast, making do instead with honeyed toast.

With the wedding over, the business of getting ready for Christmas started in earnest on Monday morning. She transferred the precious china from the dining room to the kitchen dresser. The bookshelf, still with spindles from last year's tree, was cleaned and dusted. She decked the shelves with cards and holly, fah lah lah lah lah, lah lah lah lah. The wreath was hung at the front door and the mistletoe was tied with a ribbon in the hall. All the old wax was gouged out of the candleholders and replaced with new candles. Her son positioned the tree and proceeded to decorate it, lovingly opening the assortment of boxes where the baubles were stored, and hanging them carefully, stepping back to look, his mathematical mind checking the balance. Her minimalist painted-twig idea never did materialize. On Tuesday she did the "mega-shop", and by eight was wheeling her laden trolley to the car. Later, with her son, she managed to combine a five-mile walk with some last-minute Christmas shopping, taking in the views and the art in Campbell Park. Things were gradually falling into place. She had had her walk and was beginning to calm. Unfortunately, she had taken her eye off the apple and caught a cold, realizing that since Thursday she had eaten hardly any fruit. Nose-blowing commenced. Thank God for quilted loo roll.

She had long ceased with tradition and brought her special Christmas meal forward to Christmas Eve. There was nothing more depressing than sitting down to eat with her family who were so uninterested in what they were about to receive because they were tired and hung-over from the night before. It all seemed a pointless waste of her time. Big silent tears would spill over her cheeks as she scraped the plates of unfinished food into the bin, which had to be the ultimate insult. She overcame her sadness by changing the day of the meal and for many years now it had heralded the beginning of the festivities. Christmas Eve was truly the best day, full of magic and expectation, like a present waiting to be opened, neatly wrapped, tied with a bow and given with love. There were braggarts in her step and she was filled with promising optimism. Nothing was too much trouble. If it all fell flat on Christmas Day, so be it. Preparations lasted all day, rearranging the furniture, rolling the roulade, basting the birds, making the soup, remembering to remove the pâtés from the freezer.

This year her special meal on Christmas Eve had a name. It was called The Bird Table. A whole range of feathery friends were roasted and served on ashets along the length of the table and consumed with lashings of alcohol. The event lasted way into the night.

Until "ashet" was underlined with a zigzag of red, she thought there was such a word. However, it wasn't in any of the dictionaries. She had known the word all her life: her mother had used it frequently. Fortunately, she had received a Scots dictionary as a Christmas present and looked it up. It was defined as an oval serving plate, especially for a joint. In a nutshell. She looked up "braggart", sure to be in the Scots dictionary. Alas, no. She and her husband were given the most wonderful picture of their children, taken outside the church only the other day. She could tell that her son, who had made it and given it, felt extreme pride and joy, as though he had been commissioned on behalf of all his brothers to present the work. She too remembered making presents, even as late as Christmas morning: while the children were playing, she would launch into making a new dress for her mother and give it to her later in the day. Such was her energy.

The rest of the holiday slipped into place. After the busyness of Christmas, she felt quiet. There was no let-up in the cold weather, and it continued to grip like a vice. Her son lit fires in the garden and they sat outside in the bitter cold, having various mini-meals, stoking and burning, feeding the fire's ferocious appetite, their faces glowing and their backs cold. Flurries of dust and flames rose on the cold damp air. Sparks leapt and their chair legs crunched on the gravel as they tried to reverse, flapping their arms around to disperse the fallout.

She sat deep in baths brimming with bubbles and had butter on her toast in the mornings.

Various stages of man presided over the football matches around the country, their motor mouths silenced by her husband pressing the mute button on the remote.

Realizing that she had been using milk past its use-by-date, she wrapped against the pressing cold and walked into town. Her husband insisted that she buy a bottle of wine for New Year's Eve. To be honest, she was happy enough scanning the shelves, reading the labels, dreaming of faraway places. However, to please him, she bought an Australian white, along with four pints of milk. Not making good use of her time was annoying her, and all too soon, the much-needed holiday was falling away and Monday morning was edging nearer. Livi and the rappers would be in her room again, and she would have plenty to think about then. Already wishing for Friday 3rd April.

She had not heard the explosions or seen the twinkling arcs breaking beneath the scattered light. Rockets had landed in the garden. She saw them in the morning, their exploding magic spent, lying bare and awkward on the frosted grass when half the world was still asleep. Happy New Year.